HIS TO TAKE

NEW EARTH
BOOK ONE

SELINA COFFEY

SUMMER COOPER

LOVY BOOKS

February 20, 2020

Ann stared out of the window of her father's SUV and wondered if anything would ever be the same again. Two hours ago, the ground shook, sonic booms rang around the world, and then... everything turned to chaos.

She thought about it now, as her father sped down the highway, how she'd been on the couch, watching Netflix as she waited for her neighbor, and one-true-love, Rex Wolfson's baseball game to start. It had been a normal Friday evening, and she'd planned out a new strategy to get Rex to notice her as more than just his neighbor when the ground started to shake. That, in itself, wasn't really eventful; they lived in California after all.

It was the strength of the earthquake, the way the house swayed and jumped that made them all panic. Then the sonic booms started. Not just one but several, maybe seven, Ann couldn't really remember. There'd been screams, the sound of wood and glass breaking, and so much noise that Ann screamed along with whoever else it was that screamed in the kitchen.

Now, she sat beside Rex, her parents were in the front of the SUV and her dad pressed the SUV's engine for every bit of speed it had, with Rex's parents in the very back seat. Fear, shock, and despair mingled in a rather unsettling way with the joy she found with Rex beside her. She was terrified, and even the sound of her favorite band, Fleetwood Mac, didn't calm her. She had the band's albums on her phone, earbuds in place to block out the reality of the world around her, but she still didn't feel calm, though.

Instead, she felt as if she was on the verge of dying. Her chest was tight, and her heart pounded in her chest, but this time it wasn't because Rex was there with her. Normally, when he was around, her heart would flutter in her chest, her cheeks would go warm, and she'd hide behind her long brown hair until she could breathe normally again. This was something so much more than that. It felt as if her heart had been squeezed in a vice and whoever had control of the vice just didn't want to let go.

Ann's attention was caught when her mother slammed her fist into the side of her husband's seat. Ann pulled out her right earbud, alarmed at her mother's violent display. Mary Adams was 35 years old, and except for Mary's blue eyes and blond hair, was an exact copy of her daughter. She was soft, sweet, and tender by nature, a loving mother and wife. The fear and rage now on her face scared Ann even more than she already was.

"John Adams, you tell me where we're going, and you tell me right now!" Her mother's voice was strained, not the quiet, pleasant tone that normally came from her mouth. The fact that she yelled only intensified Ann's fear.

"Mary, please, think about the children!" John reached for her hand, kissed it and sent her a calming glance with the brown eyes Ann had inherited. "It's a place up north, hidden away, where we can't be found by looters. It's a good place, and if what the news people say is true, it will be the best place for us."

"But what is it, John?" Mary pleaded, and something about the wild look in Mary's shimmering blue eyes told Ann that her mother was on the verge of a panic attack too.

Ann reached forward to touch her mother's shoulder and Mary jumped. "It's okay, Mom. Dad wouldn't take us somewhere that isn't safe."

"Ann's right, Mary," Stephan Wolfson spoke up from

behind Ann. "John told me he had a safe place for us all, and I believe him."

"But why is it a secret?" Mary whined and sat back in her seat. Like her daughter, Mary was a couple of inches above average height and her slim frame filled the front seat.

"It's not a secret, Mary, it's just hard to explain. And I'm trying to get us there quickly and in one piece." John had to swerve the wheel to dodge the SUV around a car that had stalled in the road. "We have about another hour before we get there, so just settle in and help me watch for objects in the road."

Mary just sighed loudly, and then turned the radio up.

"Ash clouds will soon fall across the country, folks." The radio announcer was male, his voice tired and sad. "This is it folks, the end of us all. Yellowstone, the Long Valley Caldera, Mount St. Helens, they've all gone off and we're getting reports that the…"

The announcer stopped to cough, and Ann's attention zeroed in on the radio. Why was he coughing?

"Sorry, folks, that ash cloud has been here in Denver for a while now." Ann could hear the man take a drink of something, and then his voice came back. "If you're listening on satellite radio, I'd advise you to get underground, now. Nobody knows how far the ash will spread, or how long the eruptions will last."

Ann knew the SUV had satellite radio and glanced at her dad. "Are we going underground, Daddy?"

Her voice wasn't very loud when she spoke, and her father didn't answer. Rather than demand an answer, she just went back to the voice of the man that announced doom for them all.

"I doubt I'll be around for much longer, folks, so I just want to say, it's been a great ride, and I hope that some of you survive this insanity to rebuild."

Ann thought it was an odd thing to say, but then wondered if it was the end of the world. But surely the ash would blow away and that would be the end of it?

Snow started to fall from the sky, and Ann glanced up, overjoyed because she'd never seen it snow in this part of California before. "Mom! It's snowing!"

"That's not snow, baby. It's ash." Her mom's voice now had that same tired edge as the announcer's, and Ann looked to the front seat. Her mom's face was tired, drawn, and filled with worry. "Don't worry, honey, your dad will keep us safe."

Ann glanced over at Rex, but he still had his earbuds in, hidden by his longish, light blond hair, and his hazel eyes were closed. The way his head bounced steadily against the window on his side would have given her a headache, she thought, but that wasn't really her concern right now.

"What did he mean, rebuild if we survive? Won't this end in a day or two?"

"It," Mary's words cut off as she muttered something Ann couldn't hear. "Nobody knows how long it will last, Ann. Science can only predict from past experiences. They can't guarantee anything. And if that many volcanoes have gone off at once? Well, maybe being underground isn't so safe. John?"

"Yes, Mary?" her father said but didn't take his gaze from the windscreen. He twitched his head when his dark brown hair, long on the top but short around the sides, fell into his eyes. He didn't even want to take his hands off the steering wheel long enough to move his hair out of his eyes. Ann thought he probably wished he'd had his hair cut now, like her mother had told him to do countless times before.

"Will it be safe underground? Surely there will be more earthquakes?" Mary's voice interrupted Ann's thoughts and brought her attention back to her mother.

"I really don't know, honey. I can only think that we'll be safe up there, and hope." John patted his wife's knee and that was when Amanda, Rex's mother, spoke up. She wasn't a geologist, or a volcanologist, but she was a science teacher at the local two-year college and knew a thing or two about Earth sciences.

"It sounds like the planet, or at least the mantel, is going through a sudden major shift, something that has never been recorded in human history. All of these volcanoes going off at once, and Yellowstone? Something's happening, and being underground might not be safe, but it will be safer than being above ground. Especially since we'll likely have something similar to a nuclear winter for years to come. Is there food there, John?"

"We'll have everything we need, Amanda, don't worry. We'll all be safe."

Ann glanced at her father and decided to try and block the world out for a little while longer. She put her earbuds in and lost herself in one of Stevie Nicks' tracks that she released without the band. It always soothed Ann, and it did so now.

A WEEK LATER, the new routine of being in the bunker was broken. The Wolfson family had started to... change.

"We'll have to lock them out of our section until they either calm down or... you know." Ann heard her father whisper to her mother.

At 15, Ann was a very intelligent young woman and had learned to listen for whispers from her parents. They wanted to protect her, to keep the truth from her, but she wasn't stupid. She knew they'd be down in the bunker for at least two years. At first, she'd been delighted. They were safe, there was ventilation, food, and the place wasn't that different from being in a house.

There were several levels, one for maintenance and the machinery needed to keep the bunker liveable, with several different technologies for energy sources. There was enough food stored for ten people to live on for 20 years on that level, as well. The level they lived on, the second level, had bedrooms for the same amount of people, three bathrooms, a living room area, a kitchen, an infirmary, and several other rooms that had different purposes. All were fitted with lights that mimicked sunlight, and there was even an outdoor area with fake grass, sun loungers, and a picnic table.

Below that was a level that had space for more rooms and a long track that could be used to walk or run for exercise. That level wasn't really complete, and Ann didn't go down there often because it was the darkest level of them all.

At first, the whole place was a little scary, but over the days Ann had become used to it, and now it felt like a sanctuary. Or had, up until the point when Rex snarled at her and his face started to sprout long, blond fur. She'd stared at him in horror as his face continued to change, and her scream had alerted her father that something was wrong.

John Adams had wrestled the young man out of the living room area and had taken him back to the left wing of the level that the Wolfsons called home. John had closed them off with the help of a heavy steel door. He'd turned on the locking system that could only be opened with a code that he knew, and he'd watched through the 4-inch tall, thick pane of glass as Rex had... become something else.

John had then come to Ann and Mary, who had rushed to Ann's side, and made sure his daughter wasn't harmed. When Ann assured him she was fine and just wanted to lie down, he'd drawn his wife over to a long black sofa on the other side of the room. Ann had sprawled out on the couch and covered her head with one of the thick green blankets they'd found piled in a storage closet. She'd put in her earbuds, but she hadn't turned on her music, yet. She knew her parents would whisper to each other now.

"Did you know this might happen?" Mary whispered to John, and Ann strained her ears to hear her father's reply.

"I'd heard a few things on the radio, but I didn't believe them. I mean, humans can't turn into wolves now, can they?"

Ann's father was a very powerful entertainment lawyer, and he knew the dark side of Hollywood and glamor. He knew that people could be evil and do stupid things. That's how he'd ended up with this bunker. A really famous actor, known as a beloved father-figure on a long-running program, had screwed up majorly and was caught in a prostitution sting down in Florida. The actor had lost everything and gave her Dad the bunker as payment for his services. Dad had kept it secret from her mom because he thought she'd be angry about the trade, but, as it turned out, he was smart to do it.

"Apparently, they can, John!" Mary hissed angrily. "We shouldn't have allowed them down here; they're dangerous."

"It's not like we knew this would happen! They've been our neighbors Ann's entire life, Mary, what could I do? Leave them to die up there? You don't know what it's like… the things I've heard about." John ran the communications room in the bunker and often spoke with others with the devices left in there. Something called a ham radio or something.

Ann had no idea what a ham radio was, and she couldn't get wi-fi down in the bunker, so she couldn't Google it either when her dad whispered about it. She imagined a ham with two wires stuck into it, bouncing around on a table as electricity ran through it. The idea was stupid, and she knew it had to be an acronym or something.

"What did you hear?" Mary asked quietly, as if afraid to hear the answer.

"This has been happening from day one. There are theories that something either melted out of an ice cap or something was kept in a pocket underground, some… I don't know, organism that can change DNA, a bacterium, or a virus maybe, or maybe even a fungus. Nobody knows, they just know that it only started to happen after the events started. People started to turn into wolves."

"That can't be true, John! Werewolves? No, I refuse to believe it!" Mary laughed, and Ann winced on the couch. She'd seen what Rex had started to become, her mother hadn't.

John pulled Mary up and guided her to the door outside the living room and showed her the small window in the door. "John! There's a wolf in there! It will kill the Wolfsons!"

"No, Mary, that's Rex. That's our new reality."

"But John…" Mary started, but let the words die off. What could she say?

"They'll calm down in a day or two, go back to their normal selves. We just have to keep them locked up until they change again. Then, we'll see what happens from there."

Ann, still on the couch, knew her parents would go quiet now as her father comforted her mother. For a moment, she longed to be back at home, with her small circle of friends, Elizabeth and Maria. They were likely dead, Ann thought, but she didn't know. They might have survived. But for what? To be slaughtered by werewolves? The thought disturbed her far too much and she did the only thing she could do now. She hit play and let the world slip away.

2

February 20, 2025

"I don't think it's a good idea, John. I really don't." Amanda Wolfson leaned back in the steel utility chair in the conference room and stared out at the rest of the bunker's survivors. "We have at least another three years before the air even starts to clear a little bit. Sending one of us out there right now, well, it's just not the smart thing to do."

Ann tuned the others out and continued to draw in one of the notepads that they still had thousands of. She wished her phone's battery hadn't died for the millionth time since that sad day and doodled instead. Rex had noticed the sky seemed lighter when they all got up that morning and that discovery had set off the current debate.

They all sat around the long, rectangular table, one family on each side, and did what they always did in a time of crisis… they discussed their options. Or, the parents did anyway. Rex and Ann rarely had any input into what happened, even though they were now 20 and 21. Another thing that hadn't changed was how much Ann loved Rex.

She cast glances at him as she doodled on her pad, hidden behind the long curtain of her hair. She hadn't cut it since they'd come down to the bunker and it was now well past her waist. The perfect way to hide the fact that she looked at him often. For all that he noticed, she thought with a sour grimace aimed at the notepad.

She'd grown into a rather womanly figure, with breasts that would fill his hands and then some, and hips that would perfectly match with his. At least, they did in the hot dreams she had about him, the ones that had led to her closing her door at night, not long after they'd moved down to the bunker. Something she'd never done in her real home.

She was embarrassed by the dreams; afraid she might do… things or make sounds in her sleep that would alert the entire bunker to where her dreams had taken her. Usually into Rex's arms, those strong arms he kept fit by spending a lot of time climbing around the bunker levels, using the weight machine, and running every single day. Ann wasn't so avid about exercise, but she ran every day, just to keep in shape.

She'd long ago given up on the idea that they'd ever leave the bunker. She had become disillusioned by her talks with Amanda about reality and the truth of their situation . She did want to stay fit and attractive for Rex, however. One day, he might notice that she could be more than a little sister to him. After all these years, and his constant moodiness, she knew she was the one for him.

And she understood why he was so… gloomy. He'd been a state champion, even at 16, and had been on his way to a glorious university career and then on to the big leagues. Everybody in town had known it, and that had all been snatched from him on that day. The day all of their lives changed.

"Have you heard anything on the radio?" Stephan, Rex's normally silent father, asked. He never had a lot to say, but when he did speak, he had a point to make. The red-headed man, with the Irish green eyes, was a writer and an academic who had taught literature at the university. He wasn't much help in an apocalypse, but he was an intelligent man that liked to clean.

"I heard something from that family up in Vancouver. They said the sky is brighter there, too," John replied, his voice tired. Ever since that day, his voice always seemed to be tired, Ann thought and glanced at him.

Her father was only 43, but he looked older. He had the burden of the entire bunker on his shoulders. They'd all offered to take over some of the roles he filled, but he didn't want to burden anyone with the problems he took care of. He wasn't the leader, as such, but he owned the place and felt responsible for all inside.

"What do you think it means?" Mary said from her place to the left of Ann's father.

Ann sat on his other side, quiet as always. It had become habit and hadn't changed over the years. Rex moved on his side of the table and she looked over at him.

His mother cut his hair the best she could, and it was cut close to his scalp. He was still as handsome as ever, the all-American boy with soft, smooth skin and eyes that made her burn. Even if he rarely looked at her.

She knew she was hopeless, but she was the only female his age in the bunker. Even if he suddenly got a case of the hots for Ann's mother, she was taken. So, logic dictated that he would eventually have to show some interest in her. Right?

Not for the first time, she wished there were normal clothes in the bunker. All they had was a lifetime supply of dark blue coveralls that they all wore every single day. White, cotton socks covered each pair of feet, and they all had a pair of Nike running shoes or black, leather combat boots. There was nothing stylish or feminine in this hellhole, and Ann knew that for certain. She'd checked more than once.

"The wind might have changed," Amanda spoke up after a quiet moment of contemplation. "Or the sun might have burned through the ozone layer. I'm not sure. Nothing like this has ever happened in recent memory."

"So, it could be clearing?" Rex spoke up and leaned forward eagerly. His earbuds had popped out of his ears and dangled down his chest. Ann stared at them, envious that his phone still charged.

"It could be, yes, son. But we don't know that. Or what the atmosphere is like now. The ventilation system and filters keep our air regulated, but up there? It could be totally different."

"How can we find out?" Rex shot back, eager for answers now that he had hope.

He'd spent the last five years either down on the bottom level working out, or in his room, staring at the walls morosely. Ann had tried to cheer him up the first few months after they arrived at the bunker, had tried to get him involved with card games, or other things they could do together, but he'd just murmur a refusal and turn to his wall or go down to the lower level. She'd stopped trying after a while.

This was the most animated she'd seen him since his father had dragged him to their lawn after the first earthquake. He'd been bitching about having to get to his game, but his dad, quiet even then, had shaken him like an errant puppy and told him to be quiet.

"Well, one of us will have to go up. Take a sample that I can test in the mini-lab we have down here." Amanda had kept the lab in working order since they'd come down.

None of them ever mentioned those times the Wolfsons lived up to their surnames and turned into wolves. They just lived their lives, helped each other out, and waited for whatever might come next. Ann often felt as if they were all on hold, waiting for the day they died, or for the day they could leave the bunker. She'd only ever wanted Rex's attention, and to her, being in the bunker was the best place for that to happen. All she waited on was the day he'd notice that she was alive. Which meant she lived her life waiting, too.

"Which one?" Rex asked, his voice breathless now.

"You don't think our old lives are up there waiting for us, do you?" Ann asked, suddenly. The idea had occurred to her, and when Rex glanced at her with an expression that screamed surprise, she knew that was exactly what he thought. "You're joking, right?"

"What do you know? None of us know what really happened up there. We've only had your dad's word for what's going on in the world. Maybe he's insane and keeping us all down here for his own sick pleasure. We don't know, do we?" His voice, deeper than it was when they came down to the bunker, was strained now, almost hysterical.

"You can't say things like that!" Ann's mother shouted at Rex, but his mother was already there, smacking him on the back of the head.

"Don't be stupid, Rex! You've seen it out there! The snow, the ice, the constant darkness! Do you really think anything could survive out there, much less our old lives? Do you think John kidnapped us all after an earthquake and has been pretending the world is doomed ever since? I thought you were smarter than that!" She glared over at her guilty-looking son, and I had to admit, even I was a bit miffed about the childishness of his outburst.

He was 21 years old, he should have been more mature than that. To think something that awful. "How long have you thought that?"

It wasn't a question, it was a demand, and he looked over at me. "I missed the game, Ann. We could have still had the game."

"There was ash falling out of the sky, you idiot!" Stephan barked at his son. "Our house had just caved in around us! Did you think he orchestrated all of that?"

"No, but I do think he took advantage of the situation. I think he…"

John's face, lined with age now, with dark circles under his eyes, was one of total shock and he interrupted Rex's tirade. "I assure you, Rex, you and your family would not have been my first choice had I known what was coming."

It was the first time any of them had ever really said hurtful things to each other, and now that Rex had started it, well, it appeared John wasn't going to stand for it.

"What's that supposed to mean?" Rex snarled and leaned towards John menacingly.

"It means that you are all but useless, even in your human form, and the only real duty you perform is to stare out of the porthole to the world above all day. Your parents are extremely helpful, they perform a multitude of tasks, and your mother has even studied the medical books to keep us all healthy, but you all do have that tendency to turn into wolves every few weeks."

Rex glared at John but didn't say anything else. It was hard to argue against the truth, Ann thought with an angry glare at Rex. What had gotten into him? Did he really think her dad was some psycho like he claimed?

"I don't think this was the direction any of us had planned to go." Mary broke into the conversation and leaned forward to look at the family across from her.

"Amanda, I respect your opinion, and if you say we wait and see what happens, I think that's what we do."

The tension left the room, just like that, and Ann wondered again at her mother's ability to diffuse a situation. She always had that ability and Ann admired it. Especially in these cold, gray walls that surrounded them in the conference room. She decided to leave them to it and head back for the living room area and out to the outdoor patio. It wasn't really outdoors, or a patio, but close enough.

Let them argue and call each other names if that's what they wanted but she'd read one of the thousands of books that populated the library. Most were non-fiction, how-to books and textbooks, but there was some fiction. She'd spent a week counting them all around the second year they'd been below ground, and she'd learned there were 50,233 books in the library. It wasn't a tiny room, after all, and it kept her busy.

There'd never been a lot for her to do down here. She'd help her mom wash clothes in the morning, since breakfast was only a matter of pouring hot water into a bag and leaving it to sit. The bags even came with biodegradable spoons, so there wasn't any waste either. They'd put the bags in a collection bin, and her father would take them off somewhere eventually. They scrubbed clothes in buckets and hung them in one of the empty rooms on their floor to dry. Amanda would help when she wasn't studying her medical textbooks and would always help her father with any science-related problems too.

If the ventilation fans weren't as efficient, she'd go down with him and check the problem, or if they needed to mix new chemicals for the chemical toilets, then she was the one to do it. Her husband kept an inventory of everything and helped to keep the place tidy. The hardest job down there, really, was laundry, and it never took long.

Because of that, Ann spent a lot of time reading and daydreaming. She'd draw pictures from her life before that day, and of the life she wished she could have. Rex featured in most of them, which is why the notebooks were either locked up in a metal box in her room or with her.

Ann had matured over the years, but in many ways, she was still that girl full of hope. She knew that, and she knew her parents knew about her crush on Rex. It was hard to really hide it in such close quarters, but she tried. At the age of 20, she knew she should have been looking forward to a career and a life of her own. She'd planned to go to the closest university she could, and then to go into a career. But even now, she wasn't sure which career she'd have chosen.

"Are you alright, Ann?" Her mother's voice came in

from the living room area and Ann turned a smile on her face that revealed two slightly crooked front teeth.

"I'm fine, Mom. Just... tired today. I didn't sleep well." It was only midday, by her father's calculations, but she wanted to go to sleep and dream this day away already.

"I didn't either, which is probably why I was so short with Rex." She sighed and sat down beside her daughter, a grim expression on her face. "That boy just makes me so mad, sometimes."

"You know he doesn't mean any of it, Mom." Ann sighed and looked away. "His entire life was ripped away before he could even live it."

"We all had that happen to us, Ann," her mother retorted but then winced. "I'm sorry, I didn't mean to snap."

"It's alright, Mom. Today's the anniversary, isn't it? We've been down here five years now, and it's just a bad day for all of us."

"I know. It's just..."

But a shout from the hallway interrupted whatever she might have said next.

"The sky is blue!" Her father's voice shouted from the stairwell that led up to the first level.

3

"Blue sky?" Ann called out as she and her mother raced to the hallway. Her father's haggard face stared down, relaxed into a smile that softened the lines and dark circles beneath his eyes.

"It's, it's some kind of miracle!" The Wolfsons soon joined them, and everybody piled up onto the deck, where they could look through the thick, sealed glass to the sky above. If you stood on the tips of your toes, you could see some of the world, edged in ice now. John held Ann up to the glass and she saw real, actual sky.

"Dad!" she gasped as he sat her down to hold her mother up. "The sky is clear!"

"I know, honey. Let the Wolfsons have a look."

In the distance, even from the back of the group of people she now stood behind, Ann could see dark clouds fading away before they disappeared. Rex suddenly broke away from them all and headed down the hall, purpose in his stride.

"What are you doing, Rex?" Amanda called out, but she knew already. He was headed for the hazmat suits. "You can't, Rex, not yet! Just wait!"

"I can't, Mom. We might not get another chance to see the sky like that, and I want out of this place, for good!"

"No, your father and John can go out, but you're staying here!"

"No, I'm not." He walked away to the closet where the suits had been stored and took one out.

"It might still be really cold up there, Rex..." she started, but he turned to her.

"I don't care, Mom. I want out."

"Well, if your father..." but Stephan just walked by without a word to pick up a suit of his own.

Soon, John was there too, and the women were all told to go down to the safe room on that level. It would keep them out of harm's way when the men opened the hatch and climbed the ladder to get out. They wouldn't know what was happening, the window only allowed so much of the world to be viewed, but if the men didn't come back, they would know it was still too dangerous to go outside.

"Maybe you shouldn't all go, John," Mary tried to say, but her husband stopped her.

"I have to go, Mary. I need to see if it's safe to take you and Ann out, don't I?" He ran a glove-covered finger down her cheek. "The suit's heaters will keep us warm, we have oxygen tanks inside, and we know our way back. We'll be fine. Besides, I'm the only one of us that knows how to take the samples we need."

"Fine. But I don't like it." She turned away, but Ann smiled as her father pulled her mother back into his arms and bumped his head against hers. They were always so sweet together. "I'll be back soon, my darling. I promise."

Ann's heart melted and she longed for Rex to say something similar, but she knew he wouldn't. She just stood there, awkward and still a teenager in many ways. She was naïve to the world, inexperienced, and sheltered. Literally. But she knew she loved him and decided that maybe she was brave enough to ask one thing.

"Dad, I'd like to go too, please." She said it quietly, but her father heard her. And so did Rex.

Before John could answer, Rex burst out laughing and pointed at her with derision.

"You can't go up there, Ann. You're just a weedy woman that couldn't lift a tree branch if it fell on you." He bent over he was laughing so hard, and didn't see Ann wipe a tear away, or the look her father gave him. "I've heard it all now. Women that want to act like men. I can tell you now, Ann, we've left that world of feminist hogwash behind."

Ann's hurt lurched in her chest as she watched him walk away, and she really wanted to tell him what she thought of him, but her father tilted her chin up and bonked her on the head with his glass. "He's just a stupid boy, honey, don't let him get to you."

"Be careful, Dad." She sniffed and waved goodbye to him.

Her dad might dismiss Rex's words, but they'd hurt Ann, deep down inside, and she hated him for a second. He was always so arrogant, the boy that other boys wanted to be, and in school, he'd been the most popular guy in their county, much less their school. He'd been known across the state for his sports abilities, and his handsome face.

He had the kind of face that would make movie stars drool, and he knew it. That had never bothered Ann. Not until now, when chauvinism was added to the mix. She wanted to tell him off, tell him how stupid he was, but she didn't. She just went to the couch in the room and tried to read while they waited.

It was agonizing, waiting on their return, and the women left the safe room to go down to the next level an hour after the men left.

"They've been gone a long time," Ann finally said after the second hour.

"They're just exploring, sweetie, don't panic," her mom told her.

"I wish…" but she didn't finish, there was no point.

"Next time, if it's safe, you can go next time."

"Fine." Ann rolled her eyes at her own stupidity and went back to the book she couldn't concentrate on.

For a while, she went back down to her room and tried to sleep, but the way Rex had sneered at her, and sneered her name, kept running through her mind. Emotional pain, and something she thought might be shame, coursed through every fiber of her being every time she remembered it. Tears fell for a while, and she fell asleep, completely exhausted.

In all the years they'd been down there, Ann had been strong. She'd done her schoolwork up until she was 18, tutored by Rex's mother, and she'd done her chores without complaint. She swept and helped Stephan clean, and she helped her father with his maintenance when he'd let her. He didn't allow her to help often, afraid she'd get hurt and they'd have no way to help her. But he'd let her carry tools when he needed to work quickly and didn't have enough hands to carry everything.

She did the women's jobs and the men's jobs, it didn't matter, so long as she stayed busy. She never wilted in her bedroom and cried over the world that was gone. It was gone, and she was sad about that, but she knew that that life was over. She had her father's brain, her mother had often said, pragmatic and logical.

Yet, she was still that romantic girl underneath, the one that had always loved Rex. And he'd hurt her deeply. She'd forgiven his laziness, for that's what it really was, she could admit now in her anger. She'd excused him for all these years, but he'd actually enjoyed having everyone wait on him hand and foot, while he mooned for five years for a life that would never be! Five freaking years!

The fact that he sometimes turned into a werewolf didn't bother her either. It frightened her at first, but the family had learned to sense when an episode was coming on and they'd lock themselves away. Over the years, the feral animals they would become had also become tamer, and the need to lock themselves in their own quarters dissipated. Sometimes, Rex would still lock himself away, but his parents would often sit with Ann's family, as wolves, and wouldn't cause problems at all. Amanda even came to Ann for petting sometimes.

The first time that had happened had been odd, and it had taken a lot of courage on all their parts to let the wolf family out in their animal forms, but it had become a part of their reality over time. At first, they'd all been rather freaked out. The Wolfsons wanted to leave, terrified they'd somehow get out and kill the Adamses in their sleep, but over time, they'd all learned to accept it. As they'd learned to accept so much already.

Ann even found it a little dangerous, in a romantic way, that Rex sometimes turned into an animal. What other form should a bad boy take but that of a wolf, she'd wondered after a while. It was only natural that he'd become something like that.

The adults had discussed the entire matter at length, more than once. Her father, always the caretaker, had refused to let the family leave. They'd have died almost instantly if they had, and he couldn't have that on his conscience. They'd all talked about it and had decided that it was safer for them all if the family stayed, even in their animal forms.

Rex hadn't liked it, he'd wanted to go, even back then. He'd thought their animal forms would protect them, that the new ability had given them some kind of special powers, but it had never been proven. And as his mother had pointed out to him, what would they eat, even if the cold and the changes in the air didn't kill them?

The Earth had shaken for eight days after the event. The bunker had just rolled with the tremors and had never shown any sign of damage. That had been a relief to them all, but they'd all wondered what had happened outside. Was there even a world left out there?

Amanda had reminded them all that the atmosphere had likely changed if that many volcanoes had gone off at once. The atmosphere would be different now, composed of far more gases that might make the air unbreathable. That had finally convinced Rex to stay put. For a while, Ann had wondered if Rex would try to run away from the bunker, but that reminder had settled that question. If he couldn't breathe, he'd die, so it was pointless to go out there. Even if he took all of the available oxygen tanks, which he couldn't possibly carry, he'd never make it to somewhere with more *oxygen* before he ran out.

Rex had only become more complicated, more morose, as time had gone on, and in Ann's mind, he'd become a tragic, romantic figure. He was misunderstood, and he had been taken from everything he'd known. Of course, they all had, but that didn't matter. She'd have lived underground for the rest of her life, and probably would, if the air up there was unbreathable. She'd endure it all because it meant she was close to him. And he'd thrown all of that right back in her face with his snide little remarks earlier.

Even in her sleep, the scene at the hatch disturbed her, and she relived the moment until her out of control emotions woke her up. She sat up on the edge of the bed, her hair tangled around her, and quickly braided it with impatience. She used a hair tie that was nearly useless, but still managed to cling to her hair, and took a deep breath. This couldn't go on. She wasn't a child anymore, and she had to see Rex for the man he was.

Rex was a complete asshole, she decided, a jerk even, but she still loved him. She could forgive him this, but she wouldn't forget it either. Besides, if he was the only man her age that she'd ever meet in her life, well, she'd have to just get used to his ideas. Even if they were disturbing.

Feminism was dead indeed. She didn't think so. She'd give in to her parents' wishes, because they were her parents, but she wasn't about to let him run ragged all over her, just because he was a man. Not always, anyway. There were times when she knew she'd give in, just to keep the peace because she hated arguments and tension, but she wouldn't always let him push her over, either.

Or she'd try not to let him do it, at least. He didn't deserve to be treated like a king just because he'd been born with a penis between his legs. Even if he was the last man her age on the planet, she knew she couldn't let him treat her like that. She'd have to find a way to make sure he fell in love with her, but also understood that she wasn't his slave.

Which might be taking it a little far. Maybe his sneer was mockery, and he'd only been joking, she decided. Her nap wasn't exactly peaceful, but she did feel a little bit better. She had never been the type to sit and cry anyway, and she would have to make that her last pity party, she decided. She headed back up to the safe room and found the two mothers in deep conversation.

The air down here was still, even with the ventilation fans, and she felt almost suffocated as the hours passed. By the time the little window had gone dark, all the women were pacing. Each one stared up at the window and hoped for some sign of the men.

"What if the air was bad?" Amanda said. "Or one of them fell and got hurt?"

"I'm sure they're fine. But, well, I wonder if it's still cold? Even with the sun shining earlier, it must have still been cold."

"Do you know? When I looked just before the sun set, I could have sworn the ice and snow were gone."

It had been snowing for well over four years now, it seemed impossible that the packed snowfall could just… disappear.

"That's impossible, surely?" Mary asked.

"The sky cleared in a day, Mom," Ann reminded her, and Mary nodded.

"You're right."

"What do we do?" Amanda asked, and they all looked at her. Mary was about to answer when a noise from above told them the hatch was about to open.

The women all ran back to the safe room and waited

for whoever had come back. They were all nervous, on edge, as they waited. Had they all returned? Had something gone wrong and somebody left behind, is that what had taken so long? When the safe room door finally opened, and all three men walked through, the women all but leaped on them in relief.

"Ladies! It's okay, we're fine," Stephan called out as he got a hug from Ann, Mary, and his wife. "You won't believe what's happened out there."

The men had already removed their suits, and they all made their way down to the lower level to have some dinner from a bag. Ann heated water as the two mothers prepared some powdered mix drinks for the families to have with their meals.

"It's amazing," John finally said after a few bites of food. "It's all… gone."

"What do you mean, it's all gone?" Amanda said, her eyes bright with excitement.

"Just that," John replied after he wiped his mouth. "The snow, the cold, the bad air, it's all gone."

"We took our suits off," Rex said around a mouthful of reconstituted beef stew. "It was still a little chilly out, but by the time we made it back here, it had warmed up. Can you believe that?"

Ann looked at the other women and knew they were thinking the same thing. This couldn't be right. The skies had cleared, the snow had melted and there wasn't any flooding?

"The ground must have been soaking wet," Mary chimed in, but the men all shook their heads.

"The ground was moist, like it would be after a light rain, but it wasn't soggy at all. We searched for hours and didn't find one sign of flooding. It's all… normal again."

"And none of you find that strange?" Ann asked, her eyes on them all now. "What, do you think some god came down from the heavens and magicked it all away?"

"Well, no, Ann," John said. None of them had ever been religious and hadn't brought any kind of beliefs down into the bunker with them, but they kept using words like miracle, and our prayers have been answered. Yet, none of them prayed, that she knew of.

"What else could it be?" Stephan asked. He'd always been the quiet one, the most contemplative of them all, and Ann turned to look at him.

"Aliens? I don't know. Maybe the volcanoes stopped, and a new jet stream started up, finally."

"It would still take months, maybe even years to melt all of that snow, Ann," Amanda, the most scientific one them all, chimed in. "It could be something that someone on the other side of the Earth has done. I don't know what exactly, but it's possible."

"But not aliens, or god, or some unknown goddess, because feminism is dead, right, Rex?" She couldn't miss that chance to rub that into him.

"Well, yes, Ann. I would think that women taking on

classic roles again would be obvious." He smirked at her, and she wanted to hate him, but his smile took the sting away. "It can't be gods, though, unless they wanted to get rid of everything and start all over again."

"You can knock that nonsense off right now, buddy," his mother said and glared at him. "You might be taller and bigger than me, but I can still take a baseball bat to you. Don't forget, I'm the one that used to play catch with you and taught you which end of a bat was which."

Stephan had always been too busy, caught up in writing his books, to play with his son, but Amanda had always been there for him, which was why it sounded so odd to hear him spew such nonsense about women's roles and their places. His mother had been a shining example of what women could do, with her athletics and her job as a science teacher.

Ann tried not to roll her eyes at him but saw that he'd astonished even himself. Did he really think that could happen? She'd never been raised to believe in creationist stories, but she could see now that he was thinking about it. Her lips pursed and she looked away. She couldn't fall out of love with him in the span of a few hours, could she?

This sudden feminist urge she had was sparked by his words, though. She'd been complacent, forgiving, and understanding of him throughout all of these years.

Life had changed, all over again, and she wasn't sure she was ready for it. She hadn't been the last time, but back then, she'd been young, too caught up in happiness at being so close to Rex to give in to shock and despair, but now? She wasn't sure she actually liked him, right now.

And she definitely wasn't sure she was ready to go outside of these walls again. It felt safe here, like home now, and she'd started to think of it as the place she'd spend the rest of her life. Sure, the food was awful, and boredom could set in if you didn't find something to fill your time with, but it was home. It had kept them alive when countless others had died.

From what her Dad had learned over the years, it wasn't just North America that had suffered with the sudden tectonic shifts that had set off the volcanoes, as many had postulated. Europe had also borne the brunt of the volcanic activity. Oddly, the Ring of Fire around the Pacific had been quiet. There'd even been reports that Antarctica had completely melted because of all of the activity. Ann hadn't known there were even volcanoes down there, but Amanda had told her there were.

Life wouldn't have been pleasant, even for those that escaped the volcanoes. The nuclear winter, caused by all of the ash spewed into the sky, had cooled the planet down significantly, and there would have been snow in places that had never seen it before. Not in this lifetime, that was for certain.

"I don't care what caused it right now, even if it was aliens," Mary said. "I just want to feel sunlight on my face again."

Ann turned to her mother. She was 40 now, the same age as Rex's mother, but without the sun damage that Amanda had suffered. Five years ago, Mary would go outside, spend her days outdoors, planting, weeding, and taking care of the home John provided for them. It was almost like a jungle in their backyard.

Amanda, on the other hand, had spent her time indoors most of the time, but when she was outside, she'd never bothered with a hat or sunscreen. Fine lines around her eyes now told the story of her life outdoors while Mary's skin was still smooth. They were good friends, despite their differences, and that was one of the reasons her father had asked the Wolfsons to come along when the world decided to rip itself apart.

"You know the first thing you'll do is find a hat, Mary," Amanda ribbed her friend and they both laughed. They both knew it was true.

"You're probably right, but to feel warmth that isn't from a blanket or body heat again would be nice." That had been a shock to them all, how quickly the bunker had heated up with them in it, despite its size. The concrete and bedrock walls just seemed to absorb every inch of heat they gave off. Luckily, the ventilation system kept it at a constant temperature.

"I'm going to find something to wear besides these horrible coveralls," Ann said, but wished she hadn't. Everybody looked at her, surprised that was what she wanted to change. But then they all laughed, and she didn't feel so bad.

"Wow, you know, you're right," Amanda said on the tail-end of a chuckle. "What I wouldn't give for a pair of jeans or sweat pants. Anything that didn't mean we had to unzip these stupid things to go to the bathroom."

"A dress and some heels would be nice too," Mary sighed wistfully. "I used to like to dress up a little when we'd go out. Hard to do here, isn't it?"

"You don't know how many times I thought about turning these things into some kind of dress. I just couldn't do it, though. I haven't sewn anything since I was a teenager, and I knew it didn't matter what I'd do, it would still look like coveralls when I finished."

"Well, you ladies can have all the dresses that might still exist. I'm looking for a pair of work boots and some trousers. Mainly for the same reason as you two." John laughed and looked over at Stephan. "What about you, buddy?"

"Books, John. Always books." He'd gone through the library, as they all had, and had even commandeered a few notebooks to write in. He hadn't been wasteful with his time, either.

"And you, Rex?" Stephan asked his son, but Rex just stood up and walked away.

"There won't be any baseball teams for him to sign with, I'm afraid," John said softly, and Stephan nodded.

"No, he's going to have to do the same as the rest of us from now on. He can't mope in his room anymore. He'll have to pull his weight out there."

"Out there? So, we're all going?" Ann asked, hope alive in her eyes.

"We'll all go tomorrow, test it out, see what it's like. Gasoline will be dead by now, so we'll have to walk out. I doubt there's any animal or plant life that can sustain us, so we'll have to take plenty of MREs, but I know there was a town not far away. We can see what's there." John wiped at his face and leaned back in his chair.

Amanda and Stephen got up from the dining table set up at the edge of the patio area and said their good-nights. There was an excitement in the air now, a hope that hadn't been there before.

"Do you think it will be safe out there for us, John?" Mary asked, her worry evident.

"I don't really know, Mary. I can't promise anything. I do know I'm tired of being in this bunker though, and if we can get out of it, even if it's only for a little while, it will be worth it, won't it?"

"I'm with you, Dad," Ann cut in, her mind already on

the possibilities of what could still be out there. "I want to see what's left."

"Then that settles it." Mary's smile spread over her face as she spoke. "We'll go. On one condition."

"What's that?" John asked, but his eyes said he already knew the answer.

"We leave this place secure so we can come back to it if we need to." She paused and looked at her husband and daughter for a long moment before she spoke again. "And we don't go more than a couple of days away from this place. I want to come back to it quickly if we have to."

"Sensible as always, my dear. I agree. Now, I'm going to bed. I have to get up early to make sure everything is ready. I'll see you both in the morning."

"Goodnight, Dad." Ann kissed his cheek when he leaned down as he walked by her. "See you tomorrow."

"That you will, sweetie."

They watched him go and then they got up. They weren't tired yet, and knew they'd need to start packing now. Mary went and found enough rucksacks for them all and they started to fill each one with the necessities. If one became lost, they'd have what they needed to survive, and the others wouldn't suffer without if it happened.

Each bag contained MREs, matches, an extra pair of coveralls, combat boots in each person's size, a pot for boiling water, a knife, fork, and spoon, toilet paper that they took off the roll, a camping blanket, first aid kits, and quite a bit more. The bags were heavy when they finished, but it would be possible to carry them with a few breaks to rest.

Their coveralls would also carry more gear they might want to take, and Ann added a couple of note-books to each bag. Paper might come in handy for a variety of reasons. Mary added a variety of hygiene products that both men and women might need, and an extra first aid kit, just in case. By the time they finished, it was late, and both were exhausted but happy with their work.

All that would need doing in the morning was to take the place offline, seal it up, and get on their way, soon after breakfast. Ann went back to her room and stared at the metal box, full of her drawings and thoughts. She had the key around her neck on a slim chain that ran down between her breasts. She didn't want to leave it all here but knew it would just be more weight she didn't need to carry.

She went through the notebooks as she sat at the piece of smooth plywood that served as her small desk. The tiny lamp was on, an old-fashioned desk lamp, but it illuminated the pages well enough. Her skill had improved over the years, and she could draw each member of her apocalypse family perfectly now. She'd learned a lot these few years, and it made her sad to leave it all behind.

A new life awaited her, though, one that had the promise of far more than the bunker life she'd resigned herself to, one where Rex might not be such an asshole, where he might even treat her nicely. That would be great, she thought as she put the notebooks away and took off her coveralls. She'd pushed the running shoes off of her feet when she came in, as was her habit. She was always a tidy person, and even if there was very little dirt down here, she didn't like to track anything into her room.

She settled under the cotton sheet and blanket with her head relaxed on the two pillows beneath them. She'd soon be outside, in the world, under the stars even. Real stars, that lit up the sky and twinkled on those below. Would Rex kiss her under those stars?

A sigh escaped her lips as she thought about the moment she longed for. Her fingers would tangle in his blond hair, and she'd melt against the body he kept in rock-hard perfection. She'd seen him running, his body was just as defined as it was when he was 16. Her lip trembled in the dark as she thought about him, about how he'd press his body to her, how he'd tilt her head back and kiss her with undying passion.

Somehow, he grew taller, and his hair turned black. And when he pulled away, the eyes that stared back weren't Rex's clear hazel eyes, they were an odd shade, an inhuman shade. They were an orange color that reminded her of an orange-colored sapphire she'd once seen at a jewelry store in L.A. As she pulled away from the extremely tall man, she realized he wasn't Rex at all.

But she was hungry for him and more than ready to give what he demanded.

5

The moment that her father opened the hatch was like a rebirth for Ann. She stared up at the clear sky and watched as the glass moved away, amazed at how beautiful it all was. All of the others went out before her and she hefted up the packs to them once they were all above ground.

It was early morning, a time she'd always loved in her life before, and she loved it now, even if there was an absence of birdsong and the noise of early morning traffic. They'd lived in a subdivision back then, full of families that commuted to the nearby city, and mornings were always busy for them all.

She could feel a breeze of fresh air across her face as she neared the top of the steel ladder embedded in the wall. What would it be like? Her father told her that the ground should be dry by now, but he hadn't said if the grass had started to come back. Was it all bare dirt with most of the plant life scoured away?

From what Amanda had told her, plant seeds could withstand some extremes, especially seeds from grasses and weeds. Would anything have started to grow back yet? She hesitated as she neared the top. Her eyes went back to the place she'd called home for all of those icy years. She was almost sad to leave it now, and for a moment, she thought about running back to her room and refusing to go out there. She'd stay, where it was safe, where she knew her place in the world, and what each day would bring.

"Ann?" her mother called down to her, and Ann's head whipped back around and up to look at her mother. "It's okay, honey. Come on out."

The smile that lit up her mother's face hinted at what she'd find above. She tapped her fingernails on the steel for a minute, a nervous habit she'd long stopped noticing, and took a deep breath. She felt her muscles relax and her heartbeat slowed. She could do this.

With a flex of her leg and arm muscles, Ann finally climbed up to the last rung and gasped. All around them was a field of grass six inches high, speckled with the occasional tree with newly formed leaves, and a few purple flowers. It was all... alive!

She finished climbing out of the bunker and stepped out into the new world, as fresh and green as they'd left.

It might have even been fresher than it was back then. Before, exhaust fumes, factory emissions, all of it had mixed together to create a smell that few ever noticed, unless it was new to them. This was… clean, natural, unspoiled by man.

"We're going to head down to the valley, check out that town that's not too far away," John said to the group as he hefted his pack onto his back.

That was when it happened, the most unexpected but wonderful thing happened that took her breath away. Rex rushed up to her with a whoop of joy and picked her up. The sudden press against her chest made her squeak, but her arms went to his shoulders as he lifted her high into the air. When he began to twirl her around, she started to laugh, even as awareness filled her. Her anger was forgotten now that she felt him pressed against her, intimately, so tightly. He let her slide down his body, and eyes the color of fading green moss mixed with golds and browns found hers.

Eyes that had always held her in their thrall, that amazed her even more up close. She forgot his hateful words, the way he'd intimated that women would be subservient in the world, all of it, as his lips moved towards her. Hurt disappeared, replaced by hunger, and when his mouth fused with hers?

Well, sometimes a kiss could be a dud. So what if there were no sparks? Maybe that came later. She was still thrilled, happy beyond belief, that Rex Wolfson had kissed her! She let the kiss go on and waited for him to finish. He pulled away, breathless and with a smile on his face that she hadn't seen in years.

"We're going to repopulate the world, Ann, you and me. It's going to be great." He moved away, picked up his pack, and started off down the hill before he'd even fitted the belt that went across his waist to hold the pack steady.

She was too stunned to move. Repopulate the world? Did that mean he wanted to marry her? She touched her lips, surprised at what he'd said, and shocked at the kiss he'd given her. The others hadn't seen it because they'd all started down the hill and she was the last one still there.

She was a little disappointed that the kiss hadn't been as explosive as she'd hoped, but it had been nice. Comforting might have been a better word. Pleasant even. But no sparks. Not like the way she felt when the man in her dreams had kissed her.

Ann shook her head, picked up her pack, and started down the hill. That had been a really odd dream, unlike anything she'd ever had before, and she refused to remember it. She watched the others as they trooped down the steep hill, and wondered why it was so easy to forget the dreams you wanted to remember but so hard to forget the ones you didn't.

She didn't want to remember that dream for many reasons. Number one would always be because of Rex. It felt like a betrayal of him, even if they didn't really have a relationship. For another thing, she'd done things in that dream that had seemed to last for hours, felt things that she didn't know could be possible.

She huffed a deep breath and caught up with her parents. The best thing to do would be to stay vigilant and watch for any signs of life. The man in her dreams obviously didn't exist, at least, not that she remembered. He'd kind of reminded her of that guy with the strange last name, she decided as they reached the halfway point down the hill.

What had his name been? Jason something. Mimosa? No, that wasn't it. Manitoba?

Her face scrunched up as she tried to remember his name, her dark brown eyes unconsciously on the lookout for danger. In the back of her mind, she knew there wasn't anything to be afraid of, there couldn't be. The world had been frozen for far too long, but there was a slim chance that something might have survived, and intuition made her scan for danger, even if she wasn't aware of it.

Something tugged at her toe, and she tripped. She put her hands out to catch herself but fell to the ground anyway. She gave a short sound of surprise but managed to roll as she fell. The pack caught most of the weight, and she was able to get up quickly. None of the rest of her group had noticed her fall, and she looked back to see what she'd tripped over. A root stuck up from the ground, a thick root that she knew must be from one of the sycamore trees that dotted the hillside.

Well, at least the world has come back to life, she thought as she dusted her hands off. Even if it nearly took her out, the thought continued, which made her chuckle softly. She sped up her pace and caught up with her parents again.

They walked until the sun was high in the sky and the heat made them roll up the sleeves of their coveralls. The building they'd spotted turned out to be a large log cabin, and they all eyed it warily from the outside. Tall trees shaded the cabin overhead and kept most of the sunlight at bay.

"The trees must have kept most of the snow off the roof. It hasn't collapsed," John said softly as they all stood there, motionless as they looked at the cabin.

A deck ran the entire length of the house, and steps led up to the landing in front of the door. It didn't look inhabited, but still, they all silently agreed that they needed to be careful.

Ann looked at it, and sadness overwhelmed her suddenly. This cabin was a symbol of all that had been lost. "All of the windows are gone."

Her somber voice broke through the silence left after her father spoke.

Mary turned at the interruption and looked at Ann. "It'll be fine, darling. We'll hang up sheets or something to close them up. It will be alright."

"I see a few sheets of plywood. We can put those up, I'm sure," Stephan volunteered.

"How long do we plan on staying here? I want to get to the town, find out if anyone else survived," Rex said as he headed for the steps. He tested the first pine step and then stepped up onto the porch. "The wood seems alright."

"Good. I guess we'll stay the night, right?" John asked and looked around at the rest of the group. "I think we're all in a hurry to find out what's going on out there."

"No, I don't want to stay here long," Amanda added and stepped up the six steps to stand beside her son. "Let's find out what's inside and settle in for the night. Even with the exercise we got on the track on the lower level, I doubt most of us are ready for more walking today."

Ann walked into the cabin and noticed first that everything was dry, even with the windows open. The air didn't smell musty either, as she'd expected it too. Now, how had that happened? Surely the snow would have got in, damaged the floors and walls, and caused mold to grow? There wasn't a single sign of water damage, however, no matter which room she went into.

"That's just weird," she said out loud, without actually meaning to.

"What's that, baby?" her father asked as he came into the kitchen behind her.

"There's no mold or mildew, it's all dry. Shouldn't it be damp after all those years of snow?"

"It is strange, now that I think about it," John mused and looked around the room. "I don't understand what's happened, and I won't pretend to, but yeah, it's strange. I guess we just have to get used to it."

"To the strangeness or being outside again?" she prompted and watched as he thought about it. His face revealed how tired he was, and she worried about him because of that. Yet he seemed energized, despite the way his shoulders sagged. Hope could do that to you, she figured.

"Both, I think. We don't know what's caused this shift, or how long it will last, so we'll just have to deal with it all as we go along. Come on, let's get some hot water going so we can eat."

Her father had been the one to remember the small camp stove they could use on their expedition and he took it out of his pack now. He set up the gas cylinder, connected the part that made the cylinder a stove, and set a pot on top to boil water in.

They all ate from the bags, gathered around the long, unfinished top of the kitchen table, and discussed what they needed to do. John and Rex worked to get the plywood up on the windows while Amanda, Mary, and Ann made sure each bedroom had sheets and covers. The lack of a musty odor struck Ann all over again.

"I don't know how the bedding smells so clean," she noted as she threw a pillow on the bed she'd sleep on.

"I don't understand it either, honey, but I'm glad for it. I hate sleeping in a room that stinks of mildew." Her mother smoothed down the quilt they'd put on her bed, and sat down. "I could stay here forever if there were windows in the place."

"It is nice, isn't it?" Ann looked around, her gaze falling on little bits of personality. A statue of Buddha, a mandala print on the wall, beads that she knew were prayer beads in a dish on top of the wide dresser. They all spoke of the person that came before her. Or at least of the beliefs of the person that owned the place. It might have been a rental cabin for all she knew.

The hours passed, and soon enough they were at the table again. The surface was rough but serviceable, and Ann decided she liked the unfinished table. It had character, like the rest of the house. She dug into her food, hungrier than she'd been in a long time. Exhaustion sank into her muscles as she finished the tasteless food she'd long ago become accustomed to. Her head turned in the direction of the living room behind her, and she stood up to make her way to the couch.

Stephan had been busy earlier, too, and had gathered up some wood to put in the fireplace. It wasn't really cold, but the fire provided light and its own kind of comfort. Ann went to sit on the pristine leather wing-backed couch and almost fell asleep slumped against the protrusion at the end of the couch.

She sat up and wiped at her face when her parents and Rex's parents went up to bed.

"Goodnight," she called after them.

Somehow, the hours since noon had slipped away, and it was dark now. She didn't think it had been that long since they'd stopped there, but maybe time had just passed her by. They'd spent some time exploring the house, done some work to make sure they were all safe and comfortable, all after a long walk. In fresh air.

Ann smiled and went to get up. Rex came out of the kitchen and his eyes zeroed in on her. He'd kissed her earlier and said something that made her heart skip again as she remembered it.

"You know, you might be the only woman my age left in the world, Ann, but you sure are pretty." He held his hand out to her, and she took it without question. He led her out onto the porch and let the door close softly behind them.

His blond head tilted to look up at the stars and she

followed his example. "The beauty of those sparkling gems up there can't match the wonder of your eyes, Ann."

"Oh, but I have plain old brown eyes…" but his lips were pressed against hers before she could finish, and she moaned in surprise.

Her hands went up to clutch at his shoulders, strong from the weight-lifting he'd kept up in the bunker. She stepped back when his legs nudged at hers until she was pressed up against the uneven wall of the log cabin.

"Oh, we're going to make such lovely babies, Ann. Please let me have you." She heard him whisper into her ear and felt something deep inside her abdomen clutch in excitement. "I want you so much. Please, Ann."

His lips trailed down her neck, and his hands wandered from her waist, up to touch her ample breasts. "Please, Ann."

Her head had started to spin, and her eyes felt as if they would never open again. She wanted to say yes, she wanted to finally give him what she'd waited so long to give, but something held her back. She pulled away, out of his embrace, but she kept her fingers locked with his.

"Not yet, Rex. Wait until we're settled, when we're not on the move and can do it all properly. Then you can have me."

With that, she slipped into the house and up to her room. She'd heard the groan of frustration he'd given when she stepped through the door. That sound made her smile all over again. She'd always wanted this, and now that she had his attention, well, she'd make sure he knew he better work to keep hers. She didn't want some quick coupling against a rough wall. She wanted the bed, the rose petals, the romance for her first time with him. With anyone.

And she'd push the memory of that man that haunted her dreams last night, the man that had her on her hands and knees as she begged for more, far, far away from her mind.

6

$\mathcal{A}$nn woke up the next morning with a smile on her face and the sensation of a warm glow in her chest. So, Rex might be a bit of an asshole, that would change over time, she was sure, as he adjusted to life outside of the bunker. He'd been cooped up in there, unable to fulfill his potential, and now, he could do that. He would change, she just knew he would.

Dressing didn't take long, and breakfast took even less time. They'd all gathered at the table and were about to go out when John spoke up.

"Do you think we should leave some of us behind, along with some of our packs? Just in case?" He looked worried but rested for the first time in a long time, Ann noted.

"I don't think it's a good idea to separate," Stephan jumped right in to say. "I think there's safety in numbers

58

and leaving the others behind could end in tragedy. What if something happens and those left behind just sit there, wondering, not knowing where we are for sure?"

"You make sense," Mary agreed and turned to face Ann. "I'd worry myself to death if you left and didn't come back."

"I'd be the same way," she admitted and looked at her dad. "I say we all go and take our chances."

"That's settled then. Good." He gathered up the now cool camp stove and carried it into the living room where their bags were packed.

Going outside again once they'd all loaded up amazed them. The grass had grown overnight, and the foliage overhead seemed thicker. And, for a moment, they all stood still.

"Is that a bird?" Stephan whispered, his eyes round with wonder.

"I think it is," Amanda replied, her eyes darting around. "It is. There!"

They all looked up as a blackbird took flight from the tree above them and flew away.

"That's just not possible," Mary whispered, fear on her face.

Her fear spread, like a sickness, and they all started to really wonder what had happened here on their once frozen planet. Could it be others from a place that had remained free of ice? But they couldn't make birds grow to full size in a couple of days! That was impossible.

"Maybe the birds have flown here since the thaw?" Ann said, and everybody looked at her with relief.

"That must be it. I knew you were a smart girl, Ann." John patted her face and walked away, leading the expedition into the unknown.

They walked for two hours, long enough for the sun to come up and the world to turn hot all over again. They'd all washed up as best they could with bottled water the night before, but didn't want to waste anymore today, so they just dealt with the sweat and the way they smelled.

Deodorant was a thing of the past. The bars had dried up long ago, and the spray deodorant did little more than fill the air with dust. Mary had suggested baking soda might help or talcum powder, but they hadn't found either one yet. Mainly because they hadn't come upon any stores yet.

They were about to stop for the day at a small house they came across, but Ann noticed taller buildings just in the distance. "That looks like the town."

She remembered it only as a passing scene in their race to escape the apocalypse. Still, she knew it must be the town, it was about the right distance away, even if walking did make it seem like the place was further away than it really was.

"That's it, if we push, we'll be there in a half-hour. Come on." John, always the natural leader, even if he didn't want to be, pressed his group for a little more effort.

Rex groaned and started to complain, but a look from his mother shut him up. Ann was too hot and tired to care what he thought, so she just kept walking. She slowed down, however, and waited for him to reach her side. "Hey, do you need some water?"

"No, I'm good." He looked straight ahead, as if he hadn't been pleading to get into her pants the night before.

"Alright. What about a snack bar? I have one cherry one left if you want it."

"I said I'm good, Ann. Fuck, leave me alone!" He sped up his pace and went to walk beside her father.

She stared after him, shocked that he'd been so foul to her again. She kept walking but her pace slowed. Some of the joy had been taken out of the day, and she just wanted to curl up somewhere and cry. But she reminded herself, she wasn't that girl. If Rex wanted to be grumpy, then he could do it all on his own. See if she'd let him kiss her again!

She had a dream man that was much better than him, anyway. Even if it was kind of sad that she'd developed a weird habit of dreaming the same man into life. The dreams seemed so real, though, and she woke up this morning with her body almost vibrating with satisfaction. She'd pushed the dream away, told herself it was because of Rex's kiss the night before, but moments from the dream kept popping into her head.

The man was huge, thick in so many places. She couldn't fit her arms around his biceps, and she had to look way up to even see his face. She wasn't short but he really made her feel tiny. And his… that part.

She felt her cheeks flame, a virginal response that she hated, but she couldn't help it. His dick was huge! And she loved every inch of it, she thought to herself, even if it was only a dream. If she thought for a second that the man was real, she'd probably die of shame about the dreams she'd had with him as the main attraction, but he wasn't, so she wasn't ashamed, just, torn.

She'd always wanted Rex, and only Rex. Her entire life for the last six years had been about Rex. She'd fallen in love with him when she was 14, long before the event, and still loved him. Right?

Ann noticed that there was a building just ahead, as she pulled her thoughts back to the present. She needed to be vigilant, she reminded herself, and not moon over some stupid boy. Man. Whatever he was.

Sometimes it was hard to remember they weren't the teenagers that had gone down to that bunker. They were adults now, and her dreams reminded her of that in ways she didn't really want to think about right now.

She stuck her thumbs into the straps of her backpack and glared out ahead. Was that building an old general store or a paint shop? She wasn't sure and slowed to look through the windowless frame.

She heard a sudden noise from her father, and he rushed back to them, hunched down. Fear pulsed through Ann's body, and she quickly followed behind her family.

"What did you see?" Mary hissed as the Wolfsons quietly sat down beside her.

"I don't know." John shook his head, his face creased with confusion. "I think they were soldiers, but not like any soldiers I've ever seen before."

They all sat there, as still as they could be, as the sounds of footsteps at the front of the building passed them by. Ann was on the edge of the building and turned her head just enough to get a look at the men.

They were all dressed in some kind of blue armor, even their heads were covered in the stuff. Dark shields of glass covered their eyes, and masks over their mouths must have filtered the air or something. For all she knew, it was to make the soldiers look even more badass than they already did, and the masks didn't have a function at all.

She didn't see any weapons but noticed odd bumps on their wrists. She'd seen enough sci-fi movies to know those could be some kind of photon weapon. Or something like that, anyway. But would anyone on the planet have that technology?

Five years after the cataclysm wasn't enough time to develop armor and weapons like that, was it? She pulled back as the men went back down the street and stared over at her family. They'd hoped to stay the night here, to maybe make camp for a while, but those men looked dangerous.

She wasn't sure why her father had ducked away when he'd seen them, but she had to guess it was the same instinct that told her those very tall, very power-ful-looking men were dangerous.

"We can't trust anyone, not until we know what's going on," her father whispered to the group, and they all nodded their heads. "I'll have a look, see if they're gone."

Ann tried not to stop him. She knew he had to look, but she didn't want him to. Fear made her a coward, and she hated it, but survival had always been the name of the game, right? Being a coward right now meant living another day, even if those men could save them and take them to a city that was still alive and well. Until they knew for sure who the soldiers were, and what had happened in the rest of the world, it was best to just avoid them.

"Let's go in the door here, get off the street," her

father said when he came back, and both families followed him inside.

The building was an old, rectangular building made of brick with a painted advertisement for Coke on the side that was probably as old as the drink was. The family made their way up to the second floor where Stephan found an office, and the family hunkered down in there. A lack of windows and a door that locked made them all feel safe, even if that safety might only be an illusion.

"What do you think?" Stephan asked as he removed his pack and sank down to the floor.

"Some kind of super-soldiers," Rex said. He'd always been an avid video game fan, and she knew he'd liked war games the best. "I've never seen armor like that."

"I didn't see any weapons," her father said, his voice confused.

"I saw some odd shapes on their wrists. I'd bet those are some kind of weapon."

"Nobody in the world has the technology for that. Especially not now, when resources would be so scarce," Amanda butted in and Ann sank back against the wall she'd slid down. Time to let the 'grown-ups' discuss and fade into the background then.

"No, I think Ann's right. I saw those bumps too," John cut in, a note of admonition in his voice. Amanda didn't have any right to talk to his daughter in such a condescending tone, his voice said.

"Well, maybe they were beacons or locators of some kind. I think we should talk to them instead of hiding in here like scared little rabbits. I'm not sure where those soldiers came from, I can't believe any society has been able to maintain any level of technological development since the event, but maybe they have. And I want to go there."

Ann had started to notice that everyone started to change since they'd left the bunker. Rex was an even bigger jerk than normal, and then he kissed her. Her father had taken on the leadership mantle he'd cast off for so long. Stephan became more verbal, more assertive when the sunlight hit his face, as if he had a new purpose in life. And her mother? Well, her mother just seemed unsettled, unable to relax, and she kept checking on Ann, as if afraid she'd lose her.

Even now, her mother's hand reached out to clasp hers and she glanced at Ann. Ann smiled and squeezed her mother's hand to let her know she was alright. Mary gave a slight nod and turned back to let her head rest against the wall.

"This is great, we're stuck in a damn office, wondering if we're about to die, when we should be out there taking whatever's left. It's our right." Rex snarled the words quietly, but everyone in the room heard him.

"It looks to me as if the soldiers have done all the claiming there is to be done, son," Stephan said, a new tone in his voice. Ann thought it might be authority. "You're just fine sitting right there. Don't go getting any stupid ideas."

"Fine. But I want it noted I voted to go back outside." Rex scowled and crossed his arms over his powerful chest.

It reminded Ann that his chest wasn't nearly as large as the man in her dreams. His was powerful, broad, and like a wall of strength. Rex was more like a little boy that wanted to emulate his dad compared to that man. She blinked quickly to dispel the memory and reached for her pack. Food would distract her.

Well, the making of it would, the stuff tasted like what it was, dried out meat and vegetables long past their first spring burst of tastiness. Eating had stopped being a pleasure when they went to the bunker and became nothing more than a function. Even the powdered drink mixes, full of vitamins and nutrients, offered little in the way of flavor now. Sometimes she'd catch the faint taste of grape or orange from the drink mixes, but not often anymore.

Rex shifted to sit beside her, and she leaned into him, despite her new reservations. He was real, solid, unlike her dream man. He leaned down and pecked her on the top of her head, and she felt a warm sensation flow down to her stomach. She wrapped her arms around him and thought that the only thing she really wanted to do was go back to the bunker.

It was safe there. They could take up their own wing, start a family, live as husband and wife, even if there wasn't anyone around to marry them now. She'd wanted to be his wife for so long and now, with those scary men out front, she was afraid she might not get that chance. What if the soldiers killed them all? She hid her quiet tears from him and swiped at them with her fist. She just wanted to go home, but she knew there was no going back now. Not yet, anyway.

7

"I think we should head out now," John said a few hours later. "I don't think we should stay here if those soldiers are around."

"No, you're right. We can walk until we find another town. There's another one not far away, isn't there? Some houses or something?" Stephen looked as if he was trying to remember exactly, his eyes far away. It had been a long time ago, after all.

"There are, yes." John nodded, and they all stood up to put their packs back on their backs.

Ann wasn't paying attention, her brain was on the soldiers, something about them had reminded her of her dream man. Maybe it was the broad power they displayed in that armor, made all the broader because of that armor. They'd been huge, much bigger than most men she'd ever come across in the time before.

With a sigh, she stood up and followed behind the others. Somewhere in the back of her mind, she knew she should be afraid; she'd seen apocalypse movies. Men were dangerous in this new world, or so movie producers always seemed to think. They would all turn into savages that treated women horribly, as she'd read in so many books on the subject. Women would become little more than cattle, as Rex had already hinted at.

She stared at the back of his head as they walked and wondered what the future would bring.

THEY SPENT two more days walking before they even caught a hint that there might be others alive. They saw the glint of a fire, quickly hidden in a dark building. It was night, and things like that would easily catch attention. A curtain must have blown around in the warm wind that blew in the valley.

It had only been a momentary glimpse, but it had been enough for Ann. She whispered her observation to her father and they all stopped to stare at the building. It was a small, two-story building with a cluster of houses around it. The sign outside had been scrubbed clean of any print long ago, but it didn't look like a shop. Maybe it was a clinic or a dental office, they couldn't tell.

"I think…" Amanda paused as they all huddled

around and stared at the building. "I think they may be like us, like Stephan, Rex, and I."

"Wolves?" Mary asked, and her gaze shifted to her husband.

There had been reports, early on, before the radio signals started to go silent, that some of the people left outside had turned and that violence from them was incomprehensible. They'd murdered those that hadn't changed, feasted on their bodies, and had then moved on. Plenty had died as the world turned cold, but those first few weeks had been a nightmare for those left outside and above ground.

"Yes," Amanda finally agreed; her face certain now. "I can smell them."

"Should we approach them?" John hissed at her quietly, his eyes on his daughter and wife.

"Let me go. I sense females, so maybe I'll be okay. You all stand ready, though, just in case." Amanda gave them each a calm smile and then walked out of the darkness behind the house where they were hidden. She looked before she crossed the street to the house, an old habit that died hard, and then she walked to the glass doors of the first floor. Somehow, the glass was intact in some of the buildings, but not in others.

They all waited, and Ann was sure that every single one of them held their breath, as the door opened slightly. Amanda said something to the person behind the door, and then the door opened wider. Ann and the rest of the group relaxed for a moment.

The wind shifted at that moment, and they all gasped as something disgustingly awful scented the air.

"What the fuck is that?" Rex gasped as he covered his nose and mouth.

"Something dead," Mary said quietly. "There are bound to be bodies of animals and, um, other things that weren't buried. Well, they were buried under the snow, but now they're exposed. It's probably best if we don't investigate."

Ann had to agree and covered her face with a scarf she'd found in one of the houses they'd searched. It was red, pink, and green tie-dye, a cloud burst of colors that she hadn't been able to resist after 5 years of dark blue boredom. She'd also found a pair of blue jeans in a dresser that fit her, and a green t-shirt that was much softer than the rough material of the coveralls. They'd all managed to find things to change into, and even if they were slightly big, it didn't matter.

She turned her eyes back to the building and waited. Amanda was gone for a very long time, but none of them had a watch and the battery in Rex's phone had lost its charge on the first day. They couldn't tell how long it had been, but luckily, Amanda came out as the other members of their group started to get restless.

"It's safe, we can go in for the night," she said as she

approached them. "There are only two old women, and they're looking after a young boy that they hid with down in the cellar. The one woman's husband died. He was some kind of survivalist and they all lived down in the basement until he ran out of his heart medicine and died. That was the only reason they knew the snow was gone. They'd come up to bring his body outside."

"Oh, that's so sad!" Mary said, and Ann clasped her hand.

"They're wolves, but safe. They aren't those feral kinds of wolves."

Ann had to wonder how Amanda would know the difference but didn't ask. The matter was private, and Ann didn't want to be rude, so she kept her mouth shut. The fact that it all sounded a little fishy to her wasn't something she was going to mention either. Two old women and a little boy?

Where had the little boy come from? Where were his parents? Dead was the most likely answer, but until she knew for sure, she wouldn't feel safe.

She had a feeling her parents felt the same way. She could sense tension in the way they held themselves, in the tightness around their eyes. Rex, Stephan, and Amanda all seemed to be relaxed, but they hadn't had to live with a deadly threat for the last five years. Not like Ann and her family had.

The Adamses had all become used to the Wolfsons

and the way they shifted over time. It was a part of their lives now, no different than getting a period or having to go to the bathroom, but from someone else?

They all walked into the building and followed Amanda back to a room that had only one window. That one was covered in a thick blanket, to hide the light from the camp-stove flames. Two small, elderly women with white hair huddled around the flame, as if it was cold, despite the warmth of the air. They looked like twins, both round with pale white skin and dark brown eyes.

You would never think they'd ever turned into anything like a wolf, they looked too sweet and innocent. The little boy was shy and hid in one of the women's lap, but Ann could see he had dark brown hair and tanned looking skin.

"This is Ricardo, my grandson," the woman on the left said. "I'm May, and this is my sister Kay."

They all said their names and then settled down. John pulled out some extra MREs and offered them to the women. "Thank you for asking us in."

"It's a strange world, now, isn't it?" May said, her eyes on her grandson. "One day, Kay and Ed, my husband, were here with me while we watched Ricardo. Juan, his father, and Amber, his mother, were at work, and then... everything just went boom."

"Yes, it was all quite traumatic, wasn't it?" Mary said from her chair beside Ann.

"I'm glad we locked ourselves down there in the basement. We've heard stories from some of the others like us. It's enough to make us go back down there in the bunker, I tell you," Kay volunteered, her eyes on the wall. "Soldiers killing wolf families and taking those that are unafflicted away to be slaves. What kind of soldiers would attack us? I ask you. Foreigners, has to be."

"Oh hush, Kay," May admonished, her eyes disapproving as she looked at her sister. "You never did like foreigners."

"Well, Juan got Amber pregnant when she was 17, didn't he?" she shot back, but a stern glance from May soon shut her up.

Not the perfect family, then, Ann decided. Not if the sister was xenophobic and the grandson was obviously half Hispanic. Sadness overwhelmed her, and she took the bottle of water her mother gave her with a tired motion. Five years and countless deaths had passed since that horrible day, and people like Kay could still carry such prejudices.

Ann had grown up with a mixture of races, she'd gone to school with, been friends with, and had learned from the other students in her school. She'd never looked down on anyone because of skin color or how much money their parents had. Students were students, just people to her, and so were the other people in her life.

"I guess you all want to lie down. It's late in the night, and we need to get Ricardo back to sleep," May said and looked over at the empty space by the wall. "This was my husband's clinic before the end came. There are exam rooms out there you can sleep in, if you want some privacy, or you can stay in here with us. It's up to you."

Ann went to stand up, ready to close her eyes and let the world slip away. She nodded at the other people as a way to say goodnight and made her way out of the larger room. It was dark in the hallway, but she felt along the wall until she found a doorknob. It turned easily, and Ann walked into the room. She could tell there were no windows, so she turned on her solar-powered flashlight and made her way to the exam table. The rubber mat was still on it, and though it wasn't made to sleep on, it was wide enough to hold Ann, at least.

She unrolled her camp blanket and settled down onto the table. Another strange day, in a life that hadn't stopped being strange since those many days ago. She stared up at the ceiling and saw that the tiles were discolored in the ultra-white of the LED light. She turned the light off, saving the batteries that were recharged by the sunlight during the day, and wondered why she'd locked the door behind her.

Was it to keep danger out? But what danger?

Rex, her brain told her. Rex was becoming a nuisance. Every night, he tried to get her to… touch him. Or kiss him, to go off to have sex with him. She'd insist that she wanted to wait until someone could marry them, then they could be a proper family, but he kept trying to persuade her.

Even last night, curled up in the darkness of a bank they'd found, he'd tried to get her to go off to one of the offices to "bang their brains out", as he'd put it. He'd said it was the perfect place, with soft carpet, and a lot of privacy. They'd all put down their blankets in the bank vault, where it was quiet and safe, and he'd said they wouldn't be heard if they went out to one of the offices.

She was too confused, upset even, by her continued dreams, to give him an honest reply. She knew waiting for marriage wasn't the best excuse, especially when there was nobody around to make it official, but it was all she could think of. She'd loved him her whole life, but now she was starting to lose some of her infatuation. Now that he'd finally started to notice her, well, she hated to admit it, but she wished he'd go back to ignoring her.

It wasn't just because of the dreams, though. His insistence on sex disturbed her most of the time. It was like that was all he wanted from her. He'd sometimes tell her he was on fire for her, or that he needed her. That he ached for her touch, and that only she could give him relief from the urges he had. She was a little flattered by it all, but she wondered if it was all a lie.

There was no love in his eyes when he said all of those things, only greedy need. She'd dreamed about him saying things like that, but now, well, she was learning quickly that sometimes fantasy was better than reality.

Ann sighed and rolled to her other side. At least the man in her dreams was honest about what he wanted. He didn't couch it in sweet lies and pretty words. He was blunt, forward, and direct about what he wanted from her. Every part of her body she had to offer.

She knew by now that something strange was happening, that the continuation of the dreams wasn't normal. With everything else that had happened in the world, and without a friend to talk about it with, well, Ann stayed quiet. It was her secret, and one she couldn't talk about with her mother or father, and definitely not Rex.

Ann took another deep breath and put her arm under her head. It was a strange world they lived in now, and she had a feeling it was only going to get stranger.

8

The parents in her group decided they'd stay another day with the elderly women and the young boy. Ann and her mother carried up the heavier things the women needed from the basement, boxes of dried food, and dozens of bottles of water, but they left some down there, just in case they needed to go back.

If there were soldiers hunting wolf survivors, then the option needed to be left open to them. The door on their basement locked from the inside, and it was reinforced steel, so it wasn't likely that anyone could get through it.

"I've heard they have some kind of laser weapon," Stephan spoke up, though they hadn't really heard from anyone other than the women since they'd spotted the soldiers.

"I've heard that too," May replied and rocked in her

rocking chair. Her white hair was a white cloud around her face, and she had her grandson in her arms. Kay was beside her, both dressed in denim jeans and flannel shirts with the arms rolled up.

"Do you know exactly what they are?" John prodded, and May's gaze turned to him.

"No, I don't rightly know," she said quietly. "I have only heard what other traveling wolf families have told me. The unafflicted tend to stay away from us. I guess they can sense us or something."

"I can't tell anything," Ann started, but her mother patted her arm and she went quiet.

"What happened to your daughter and Ricardo's dad?" Rex interrupted, and Ann noted that he'd been staring at the boy for a while now. The question was rude, and Ann glared at him. What a thing to ask!

"We don't know, like I said last night. They left me here with a baby to keep an eye on, and they never came back. They knew they could go down to the basement with us, but, well, they just never came back."

"Maybe they found somewhere else to hide, and they're on their way back now," Mary said, but they all knew there was little hope of that.

"I can only pray you're right," May whispered and patted the little boy's back. He was almost asleep, on her broad lap, and Ann wondered if he ever spoke. And why was Rex so interested in him?

"We'll be out of your hair tonight," Amanda promised and sent her own look in her son's direction.

"How can you be so rude, Rex? Stop that," Amanda hissed softly, but Ann, sitting right beside her, heard what she said.

She didn't hear if Rex replied and decided it was time to rest up for a bit. "I'm going to lie down for a bit before we start walking again."

"Alright, honey, enjoy your rest," her mom told her, and she waved at the room in general as she left.

She went to her exam room, dug around in her pack, and found a book inside. She'd started to leave the ones she had finished behind, in safe, dry places, in case anyone else needed a distraction along the way. It also lightened the load in her pack, which was a good thing. Instead of getting lighter, though, every day made the pack seem a little heavier. Some time without it on her back was heaven.

She kicked off her running shoes and climbed onto the table. She'd changed her shirt to a long, white one that floated around her upper thighs in a flirty kind of way. It was made from the same material as her t-shirt, but softer. It was something she'd have picked out at the mall for the times when she wasn't in her school uniform.

The words soothed her brain, and calm started to wash over her. Before too long, the words started to blur, and then her eyes closed. She floated somewhere between sleep and reality. She didn't react when she heard the click of her door opening, or when she heard footsteps. It was just noise, until she felt someone brush their fingers against her face.

With a stunned gasp, Ann sat up and pushed the hand away. "What the hell?"

"It's just me, Ann. Let me touch you. You looked so sweet laid there with your eyes closed." He had an odd look in his eye that made Ann nervous.

"Rex, I think you need to go back to the rest of the group," she told him and made to get up from the table. But he pushed her down, his weight on top of her a burden she couldn't budge. When he pulled his legs up and let his full weight fall on her, she could barely breathe. "Rex, you're hurting me, stop it."

"Oh, Ann, just a minute. It will only take a minute, please…" His lips were against her neck, and she tried to push him away, but he wouldn't budge.

For a moment, she gave up, she let him touch her. She'd wanted this for so long, to be his, she reminded herself as his hand went up her top to cup her breast. She had a white tank top on underneath it, but his fingers had found their way beneath that too.

She waited and let him touch her because she loved him. Didn't she? She'd wanted this to happen, oh so long ago. Maybe letting him have his way would bring that love back. Maybe it would bring back the quiet, poetically broody Rex she'd loved for so long.

She had to admit it was kind of nice to feel his lips on her. And the way his fingers played over her nipples wasn't bad. The sensation almost echoed what the dream man made her feel, but not quite. Rex's fingers gripped at her nipple then, too tight, too hard, as he bit into her neck.

It wasn't a gentle bite, a love bite to entice her, as she'd dreamed about lately. It was painful, and she cried out. This wasn't right, he shouldn't be able to do this just because he was heavier than her, stronger than her.

"Rex, stop. No. I don't want this." She pushed against his shoulders and tried to draw away from him, but he just pressed down harder against her body.

"Of course, you do, Ann. You've wanted me since you were 14 years old and started to grow tits. Don't think I didn't notice. I did, you just weren't in my league back then."

Having her schoolgirl crush, and the mention of her budding breasts, thrown in her face was like a bucket of cold water over Ann and she struggled harder. That only made him more excited it seemed, and his hands were everywhere as he attempted to hold her down long enough to get her pants off of her.

"Hold still, dammit, Ann! Stop fucking around."

"NO!" she finally screamed, and then screamed her father's name, as loud as she could.

The sound of running feet and the door opening came just as Rex jumped off of her and stood with his arms crossed over his chest. "It's alright, she thought she saw a rat."

"What?" John huffed out and looked at Ann, now sitting up on the table, her face in her hands.

She didn't want her father to be angry at him, surely it was just a reckless moment, a second of madness that had made him act like that. She screwed up her face and wouldn't look at her father as she confirmed Rex's lie.

"It was just a shadow, but I thought it might be a rat. Aren't rats and cockroaches supposed to be the only things that would survive this kind of stuff?" She even managed to huff out something like a chuckle at the end, but she wouldn't meet anyone's eye. She couldn't.

"Ann, are you alright?" Mary rushed past John and Stephan to push Rex out of her way.

Mary took Ann's face in her hands and looked her daughter over. Ann couldn't hide the tears in her eyes and brushed them away with a rueful laugh. "It was just me being silly, Mom. Nothing to worry over."

Mary's eyes slid slightly in the direction of Rex and then came back to Ann. She turned then and told the men to go back to whatever they'd been doing. She wanted to talk to Ann alone. The men left and closed the door behind them quietly.

When she was certain they were alone, Mary pulled up the utility chair the doctor would have sat in while he examined his patients. Now beside her daughter, she looked up and took the young woman's hands.

"Tell me if he's bothering you, Ann."

"It wasn't that, Mom. It was a rat," she started but stopped when she saw the look on her Mom's face.

"You've never been afraid of animals or insects, Ann. Tell me. Is Rex bothering you?"

"Mom, you know I've had a crush on him my whole life. It's normal, isn't it? Besides, we're the only people our age that might be alive. The only people we've met so far are two old ladies, a little boy, and some soldiers we saw. He might be my only chance to have a husband and family."

"That doesn't mean he gets to do what he wants with you!" Mary spat out, anger in her voice, but not directed at her daughter. "Ann, I know you were sheltered down in that bunker, but you know what sex is, right?"

"Mom!" Ann shot out, indignation laced the word. "Of course, I do, but really. I don't want to talk about this."

"Ann, if he's trying to make you have sex, then it's wrong. Even if he is the only man your age left on the planet, you shouldn't be forced to do anything with him that you don't want to do."

"It's not like that..." she tried to say, but her Mom was right. "He's changed since we left the bunker."

"He has. I know. He was always a little pri..., um, I mean always kind of arrogant. No, I take that back, he was always a little prick to you, but you adored him, so I didn't say anything. I didn't want you to be mad at me. But now? If he's trying to make you have sex with him, honey, that's wrong. That's not love or anything like it."

"Maybe I should think of it as an arranged marriage, now that he's paying attention to me," she said with a soft laugh, to try to ease her mother's mind. "I know him, grew up with him. It's better than the alternative of being alone and not having children."

"Oh, honey, that's not what I wanted at all for you in this life. I wanted so much for you." Her tone was wistful and laced with sadness. "I wanted you to get your bachelor's degree, and have a career, find out who you are, before you got married and settled down. Your dad and I were young when we got married and had you, but we knew who we were. We wanted you and the life we were building. I wanted the same for you. Not this... bullshit we've ended up with."

Ann could remember, years ago, before the end of the world came along, how her mother would sometimes swear, but she'd always cringed when she did it. Now, she didn't cringe at all. Anger at fate, at this new world, had changed them all, and Ann had the feeling her normally quiet, introverted mother was suddenly becoming someone much more demanding and in control.

"What do you think I should do, then, Mom?" Ann asked, unsure.

She'd never had a boyfriend, and she'd never been kissed, not until Rex kissed her. Her only example of male-female relations was what she'd witnessed before they'd gone in the bunker, and what she'd seen from the two sets of parents she'd been cooped up with. Both seemed to be built on trust *and* respect, something she and Rex lacked.

"If you want to take your chances, and settle for Rex, I think you'll have to grow one major backbone, and use a baseball bat on him. Failing that, you'll have to rely on your father and me to keep him in line. And I suspect his own parents. Amanda and Stephan won't let him treat you badly."

"I hope not. I'm so confused, Mom. I really don't know what to do."

"The thing you're forgetting here, Ann, is that you don't have to do anything. You can put him off, tell him no and to fuck off, or you can agree to what he wants. Either way, the choice is yours. I'd say, for now, put him off until you know for sure what you want. It's not like he has any other choice."

"You're right," she said, with a real smile this time. "I just wish he'd back off a little bit."

Ann started to speak, to say more now that they were having this rather frank discussion, but she stopped. She wanted to talk to her Mom about the dreams, but something held her back. Something told her she wasn't supposed to say a word about the man that came to her every single night in those dreams she had.

"I'm glad you came to talk to me, Mom. I still don't know what I want to do, but I feel better now. Not so alone." She pulled her mom up from the chair and the two cuddled together on their sides, spoon fashion, on the tiny padded table. They hadn't done that in a long time.

It felt nice to wrap herself around her mom. When she was younger, her mom would wrap around her much smaller daughter. Ann had always felt protected then, cocooned from the world and safely tucked away. Now, she realized her own strength and abilities. Cuddling with her mom drove home the point that she was an adult now, and she had to stand up for herself. Not just where Rex was concerned but in all facets of her life.

"You are a strong person, Ann. You always have been, baby. Don't let some stupid boy, because that's all he is still, a little boy no more mature than poor little Ricardo, drag you down. There's a whole world out there waiting for you to discover it. Don't settle for the first thing that comes along, my dear. Stay strong and find your true happiness."

Ann agreed with her mother, up to a point. She had to be sensible, strong, and logical to make it in this new world. They still didn't know a lot about what had caused the thawing, or the air to clear up, but she knew it was something major. And maybe, just maybe, there was something more for her out there than Rex had to offer. Maybe.

9

nn's feet were sore, and her thighs ached with the fire of a million ant stings. Or what she thought that many ant stings would feel like. Every part of her hurt and she had come to hate the pack she wore on her back. After a week, it would be safe to think that you should be used to walking miles every single day.

That wasn't the case, though. She had a blister on the back of her left heel that made every step sting like she'd shoved a razor blade into her foot, and there wasn't a part of her that didn't ache. They hadn't found any more people, not since the sisters all those days ago, but they had found guns, ammunition, and more clothes to trade for the old ones they had on.

"I told you those hiking boots would give you blisters." Her mother said as she dropped back to talk to her daughter. "I've got a bandage if you need it?"

"I think I do. We'll check on our next break." They'd started walking long distances during the night once they'd left the sisters behind.

Ann's father was certain that any survivors left would make their way to the cities. And if there were soldiers running around, they were more likely to be in the cities too. They weren't overly excited about running into the soldiers, but a little spying might come in handy. John wanted to know what the soldiers were doing, if they really were the enemy, and if there was a haven above ground.

They'd discussed it and decided that if the soldiers were really dangerous, then they'd go back to the bunker. Well, all of them except Rex. He was determined not to go back down there. At least he'd left her alone since that last night, Ann thought and looked up at his back.

She refused to give him any more of her thoughts right now and concentrated on putting one foot in front of the other. The nights were warm now, and she had on a pair of black cotton shorts. Not practical if a wild dog attacked her, but the shorts kept her from overheating.

"Do you think we'll stop soon?" Ann turned to her mother to answer but jumped away when bright lights filled the road they'd been following, and a voice rang out of the night to order them to halt.

Everybody scrambled. That had been the plan, and it

was a good thing too, because that's exactly what happened. Mary grabbed Ann's hand and pulled her daughter to the edge of the building they'd just walked by. Ann quickly glanced back and saw that her father was right behind them with the Wolfsons following behind him. None of them stopped to ask questions, they just ran.

Blue lights flashed, over and over again as they raced away, and Ann was sure her heart would burst out of her chest. She could barely breathe she was so afraid, but her mother pulled her behind the building, and they waited for the rest to join them. They could hear the sound of an engine moving down the road toward them, and then the sound of running feet.

They all took out the weapons they'd scavenged. Ann had a small handgun, and she thumbed the safety off as she shakily pulled it up in front of her. The Wolfsons and her father were all in the way, but she was ready. Blue lights of energy zoomed by the corner of the building. Ann was surprised when the lights started to come from all sides.

The air filled with smoke from the guns and the noise they made, but nothing seemed to stop the invading soldiers. Mary screamed when she saw a giant of a man come around the corner and pulled the trigger of the rifle she had slung over her shoulder. The bullets just tinkled away from the man as he walked towards her, and Ann unloaded the pistol in her hand.

Nothing stopped him, it didn't matter where she aimed the gun, and she screamed her horror as the man pushed Mary out of the way. Soldiers flooded in from both sides, and screams filled the air now rather than shots. It was over before Ann could take in exactly what had happened.

The soldier that pushed her mother to the ground now forced Ann to her knees. She put her hands over her head and looked around to see the rest of the group had done the same. Her father's head hung low, as if in defeat or shame, as did Stephan's. Amanda and Rex, however, glared at the soldiers.

Ann could only look around, terrified of what came next.

Mary got up from her spot on the ground and knelt beside Ann.

"You are still young enough to bear young," a soldier that had come up behind the first one said. He was looking down at Mary. "But I think you are bonded to this man, yes?"

"I am, yes," Mary said, her eyes frantic.

Ann stared at the soldier, fear a grip that tightened around her throat. They all still wore the black shields over their eyes and the masks that covered their mouths and lower face. She noticed the soldier that spoke had an accent, but she couldn't place it. She'd grown up in California, where people from the strangest places often popped up, and in the age of online videos and television, but the accent did not ring any bells.

A fresh wave of fear washed over her when the soldier spoke again.

"On your feet. This is the end of the road for you."

"The end of the road?" she squawked, but the men ignored her.

They were taken to a vehicle that looked like an odd square box, painted a bluish-gray shade. There the soldiers stood around the two families. The one that had spoken stepped forward, dropped something on the ground, and a green light appeared. It was the size and shape of an elevator, but completely clear.

"Get in," the soldier ordered and pushed Ann forward.

She resisted, afraid that the box would turn out to be her coffin, and she reached for her mother. The man pushed her again, harder, and both women tumbled into the box. Everything went quiet around them, and they looked around, now frightened beyond thought. They couldn't see beyond the faint green glow of the "walls" of the box. Tears slid down their cheeks as they clung together, wordless. Her father soon appeared, and immediately after, the ground felt as if it dropped away and they sped into the air.

Screams filled the air, and Ann dropped to the floor of the box as gravity forced her down. She thought her body would explode from the force that was exerted on her, but it all suddenly stopped, and the box stopped moving. What now?

She blinked tears from her eyes and stood up when nothing more happened. Her mother and father had tumbled back, against the walls, then righted themselves, their eyes on their only daughter. What happens now?

They were left to wonder, moments turned to minutes then to hours. Ann did not complain, though she needed to relieve her bladder, and her tongue was so dry it stuck to the roof of her mouth if she didn't pay attention. Her mother started to speak, from the place where she huddled at the side of her husband, but the box disappeared, and they could see that they were in some large hanger.

People shifted through metal guide bars that separated the place into... paddocks? That was the only word that came to mind as Ann walked between her mother and father. They were like cattle being led to the slaughter. She'd tried not to think the worst as they waited in that box, but now all the thoughts came to her, fully formed and terrifying.

Would the soldiers shoot them? Electrocute them? What would happen? And... what were these soldiers?

There was no technology on the planet that could do what that box had done, and the thought crept in, that perhaps these soldiers, these men, were aliens. Was it possible?

She distracted herself with the mystery as hundreds of people ahead of them moved forward, a dozen at a time. The way the sky had cleared, and the ice had melted, that hadn't been natural. Surely there should have been decades of storms as the ice cleared and the atmosphere changed? Shouldn't it have taken a lot longer than a single day?

Rex had implied that there had been some greater power at work, and now, as she stared around at other terrified people, covered in drab clothes and wan expressions, she had to wonder. Were these soldiers really aliens, and were they the ones that had made the planet inhabitable again?

Ann was certain her bladder would burst by the time they made it to the front of the line. A group of 12 was counted off and the soldiers pushed the group towards two entryways. A sign on each side of the doors declared one for males and the other for females. Ann was relieved when she found herself herded into a large room filled with toilets. Ann relieved herself and came out of her cubicle to find her mother. They walked out through the door on the other side of the toilets and found cups of water. They each drank two before a soldier at the other end glared and told the gathered women to keep walking.

Like quiet, obedient sheep, the women moved along a black corridor, until they reached a door. One woman would be shoved forward, a metallic door would slide down the wall, and a few minutes later, the door would open. None of them knew what happened to the women that were before them, but they all knew they had no choice.

The bathroom break and the water had appeased them all to some degree, and Ann knew they were all in shock. There were no quiet whispers, or giggles, but oddly, there were also no sniffles or giddy cracks of hysterical laughter. It was all very, very quiet. Ann, stunned into complacency up to this point, watched as the woman in front of her mother disappeared. Fear swelled all over again, and she suddenly stepped in front of her mother when the door opened.

Her mother tried to push her away, tried to protest, but Ann put her hand on her mother's arm and stared at her. She didn't speak, she just looked at her mother with all the love she could muster in her eyes and walked into the open doorway. The door shut quickly and she waited, her eyes straight ahead and her chin up. Brave until the end.

Or at least until warm air suddenly blew over every inch of her skin while a red light scanned down her body. Her clothes had disappeared and every cut and scrape she had was now cataloged on a screen that appeared in the cloud of white dust that appeared around her. She looked down to see the white dust was the very outer layer of her skin and presumably her clothes. Every dead skin cell and hair below her collar bone disappeared as the scanner searched her for injuries and health problems.

The words on the screen were in English, and she could see that she was given a fertility rating of 100%. Well, that's great she thought, and the hair removal without waxing or shaving was awesome, but why the hell did her ability to bear children matter? She could understand wanting to know if someone was ill, but their fertility rating?

That sent a new fear down her spine but all she could do was splutter as the scanner moved over her head and cool air blew at her head. Her long hair tangled in the wind, but fell down her back, clean and shiny. A new door opened, and Ann walked through it. As she did so, she felt a burning sensation on the top of her wrists and looked down.

A barcode was etched into her skin, some kind of tattoo. Her skin wasn't marked or bleeding, nor was it blistered, it was just... marked. She also now had some kind of black silk cloth wrapped around her body. It left very little to the imagination, but at least it covered her.

She didn't like being marked, but she saw no one to complain to. All she saw were people like her, hundreds of them, pressed into a solid white room with nothing in it but people. She pressed herself against a wall and waited, hopeful that her mother and father would soon emerge. It didn't take long before they came out of the doors behind Ann, barefoot but covered in the same black silk.

"Why are we the only ones in black?" Mary hissed at her husband, but he didn't answer, he just gathered the two women in his arms and sighed gratefully. They were together again.

A new door opened, and Ann and her family learned that a new waiting game was in play. Over time, they moved forward enough to see names would appear on the wall in very light pink lights, and the people on the list would move through the door.

Ann and her family waited, and soon enough, their names appeared too. They walked out to a much smaller room, this one completely black, but lit by a small lamp. There was a table and four chairs. Behind the desk was a soldier, a very large soldier, bigger even than the rest.

"You are the Adamses, correct? Father John, mother Mary, daughter Ann?" When they all said yes, he gestured at the chair. From a pile of folders in front of him, he took one marked in black. "These are your papers, your instructions, and your new address. You are a lawyer, sir, and because of that, you have been placed in charge of your part of the city."

"Pardon?" John said, confused.

"You will be moved to the city in a few moments. Your job there is to keep order, *rep*ort to us regularly, and make decisions about life in your new, shall we say, kingdom?" The soldier paused, and Ann waited, breath held, for him to continue. This couldn't be real, could it? Had that many people really survived the last five years? "For that service, you will live in a nice house, be given servants, and all that you will need. You must keep order, however. Only major problems are to be brought to us while we do the Gathering. Until the Gathering is complete, you will be the ruler of your land. But we are the overlords. Don't forget that."

The way he said Gathering told Ann that the word was likely capitalized if it was ever written. She stared at the soldier, relief on the horizon, but for now, she was confused. There was something familiar about this soldier, about how he tilted his head, and the deep pitch of his voice. But she didn't know any of them. So how could he be familiar?

10

"I don't believe this," Mary whispered as they were guided into one of those odd lightbox transporters to be taken down to the ground.

"I won't believe it, not until we're on the ground again," John said, his arm around his wife as the box closed and the ground suddenly dropped out from beneath them.

"Dad..." Ann strangled out as the force of gravity made it feel as if she was being pushed up the walls of the box.

"Hold on tight, baby girl." Her father used a term he hadn't called her in a long time and reached for her hand.

By the time the box came to a stop, they were all huddled together in a corner, and when the box disappeared, the small device that created it flew away, up into the sky. Their eyes followed the trajectory of the device and saw a huge black thing in the sky.

It was massive, beyond anything they'd ever seen in the sky before. It almost looked like a supersized, but flat, warship that the US Navy would create, but they all knew it wasn't.

"Aliens," John said, and Ann wanted to joke about the guy in the meme but didn't.

"Because, aliens," just didn't seem appropriate right now.

"Come with us now." Two soldiers brought their attention back to the ground, and the Adams family finally saw a black van with windows only in the front of the vehicle.

The Adamses climbed into the seats inside the van and watched as the city's landscape passed by. Rubble from past events was already being removed, and glass replaced in the empty windows of buildings.

The soldiers didn't speak at all to the family, they simply transported them to the center of the town, to a house hidden behind a tall, steel fence. The gate opened, and Ann almost gasped in wonder. Fruit trees, flowers, and plants bloomed with life and the house was sparkling clean.

The driveway wound up to a house that was three

stories tall and sprawled over at least an acre of land. Something told Ann there would be a pool in the back, sparkling and blue. She stared, almost numb, at it all. The aliens had done all of this, she knew it instinctively. Logic also told her it had to be the aliens. What else could turn the world around so quickly?

The van came to a stop outside the double doors made from some tropical wood that Ann couldn't name. The outside was stucco painted a tropical yellow and had terracotta shingles on the roof. A typical Californian mansion, but so far from typical it astounded her. They were going to live here? How?

They would need an army of servants to keep the place up... and just as she thought that, a man came out of the front doors, dressed in black slacks and a white, button-up shirt. He was in his late 40s, rather average looking, but non-threatening. He opened the door to the van and the family climbed out.

"Have a good day," the driver called before he pulled away.

The family watched as the driver drove away, still too shocked to believe any of this was real.

"Hello, my name is James, and I am your butler. If you'll follow me please, I'll show you inside." His smile was polite, but gave little away.

Ann wanted to explore outside, but her curiosity

about the inside of the house overcame that. The family followed James up the tiled steps and into the house.

"There are 23 rooms in Quinta de Rosa, 10 of which are bedrooms. There are en suite full bathrooms for each bedroom, fireplaces, tennis courts, the swimming pool in the back, a movie theater, a music room, and much more." James indicated that they should follow him, and the man took them into a sprawling living room filled with dark wood furnishings, and furniture covered in leather so dark it resembled dark chocolate.

One wall was little more than one long window, but each section opened up to allow air to flow in. Ann saw an antique writing desk in one corner, two long couches, three recliners, several coffee tables, and small end tables topped with white marble lamps. It was a palace, not a home, she decided. Expensive, tasteful, and luxurious. It was so far removed from life in the bunker, and in the abandoned houses that they explored after they left the bunker, that it seemed as alien as the invaders in the sky.

"It's all too much," Mary whispered loudly, and Ann moved to put her arm around her mom.

"At least we have a place here. I thought that was the end of us." Ann guided her mother to one of the couches as she spoke, and James waited for them to be seated before he broke in.

"Would you like any refreshments? We have water,

coffee, tea, and some wine. There's also some lunch prepared if you are hungry."

"Just some water, please, James," John answered for them all. "I'm afraid we'd all bounce off the walls if we have coffee after so long being without it."

That had been the first thing they ran out of in the bunker. Ann missed the flavor of a good cup of coffee but wasn't sure any of them really wanted to start back on the addictive drink right now. It was the least of their worries anyway.

"What does it mean, Dad? You're the leader, ruler, whatever?" Ann looked up to see her father on the other couch, his feet up on the buttery soft leather, still without shoes.

"I guess we'll have to look through this." John opened the file by pushing black pieces of elastic aside and pulling back a cover. The file contained three large yellow envelopes.

He stood up and handed one to Mary, and one to Ann. Ann saw that her name was on the outside and wanted to tear into it, but felt nervous about it. What role could she possibly have in this new world? She was, by that soldier's words, the princess of the castle. Quinta. Whatever.

"That soldier was right," John said after a while. "I'm basically the king in this district. I have the power to make laws, enforce them, and am the final decider in most things. There's a list of things they've kept control of, who can marry, for instance, and who gets the death penalty, but otherwise, it seems most of it is left to me." He sounded as stunned as Ann felt.

"But John, you were an entertainment lawyer, not a defense attorney!" Mary said, her eyes on her own papers, of which there were far fewer than the number in John's envelope. "I'm supposed to be your consort, and another branch of the law, should you need it."

"What does that mean?" John looked puzzled, and Ann answered for him.

"I think she's supposed to keep you on the straight and narrow. In case your new power goes to your head." Ann smiled at her father with mirth, as if he'd ever allow something like that to happen.

He'd been a very powerful man in the past, but he hadn't been cruel or overly power hungry. He'd just been efficient, and good at his job. He could work out contracts in a client's favor, fix legal problems, and file papers all day long, but he'd done it because he excelled at it, not because he'd wanted to be some kind of king of the realm. That's why they'd lived in a normal house in their previous life.

Sure, it had been in a good neighborhood, and the house hadn't been cheap, but it had allowed them all to live a comfortable life without the glamour that so many sought out. Now, they had a virtual palace, and a "realm" to run.

"This is all very strange. I don't get any of this. I don't want to be a king." John looked miserable, but Ann didn't let that go on for long.

"Dad, we're alive. A few hours ago, we were certain death was imminent. We were all terrified that we'd reached the end. But now, well, it might not exactly be the life we wanted, but it is life. On top of that, we've answered the mystery. Aliens cleaned up Earth for us."

"I suppose you're right. I wonder if they've fixed any of the optician's offices. I miss my glasses." He squeezed the bridge of his nose and Ann blushed.

She'd sat on his glasses the first year they were in the bunker and crushed the delicate frames and the glass in them. He'd left them on a chair and she hadn't realized it when she sat down, which meant it was really his fault, but she'd been the one to sit on them. It still made her feel guilty when she thought about it.

"We'll find out soon enough, I guess," Mary said and went quiet as the door opened. James silently brought in bottles of water on a tray and three glasses. Before he left, he paused.

"There are buttons in all the rooms," he pointed at a clear button on the wall on the left side of the door. "That's the call button. If you need anything, just buzz and I'll come find you."

"Thank you, James," Ann said, and he gave a curt nod before he left the room. Ann watched him go, still trying to get her head around the fact that they had servants. "Should we explore, maybe?"

"I'm too tired to do anything more than find a bed to sleep in. I'm guessing the bedrooms are all upstairs." Mary stood up, stretched, and then looked down at her feet. "I need shoes too. This is ridiculous. They can zap us with some kind of laser to clean us, but can't find us any shoes?"

Ann chuckled softly and followed behind her mother as they all climbed up the red-carpeted stairs to the right side of the house. The stairs were marble with oak railings and went up to a landing on the second floor. A hallway greeted them there with five closed doors down the length.

"Do you think the rest of the rooms are on the other side?" Mary said, but Ann knew she was too tired to care by the way her voice trailed off.

"We'll find out later. Why don't you take the first room there, and I'll see what's left." Ann kissed her mother's cheek and then her father's. The couple disappeared behind the doors, and Ann went on to explore. The first room wasn't too big, but it was open and light. The problem was that every part of it was white. It reminded Ann of the rooms on the spaceship and she shuddered.

The next room was done in blues and whites, an ocean theme prevalent in the décor. The next room was more grown up, and though Ann wouldn't have admitted it in the past, far more romantic. Decorated tastefully in reds and blacks, the room had a king-sized bed, doors that led out onto a patio, and a very large bathroom through another door. She loved the darkness in the room, it reminded her of the bunker and simpler times.

She was on the patio, bottle of water in hand, when she spotted Rex mowing the grass by the tennis court. She threw open the closet, hoping there were clothes inside, and laughed in delight when she saw the closet was full of clothes in her size. She pulled out a pair of shorts, threw on a white bra she found in a drawer in the closet, a white t-shirt featuring Stevie Nicks on the front, and then put on a pair of black flips flops.

It was suitable for the moment, when all she wanted to do was find out what had happened to Rex and his family. She ran down the stairs, through to the back of the house, and opened doors until she found one that let her outside. She'd decided to forgive everything that had happened the last couple of weeks the moment she saw him pushing that lawnmower and her love for Rex was right back where it used to be.

They were all free now, they knew what had caused the sky to clear, and life could get back to normal. She still had no idea how many people were left, but there must be a few. And her father had said something about marriage earlier, so they could actually have a real wedding now. He would go back to being the charming boy she'd fallen in love with all those years ago, now that he was free of the bunker and could get on with life as it used to be. Well, almost. Her father hadn't been a virtual king back then. Just a lawyer.

She ran to Rex and threw herself into his arms, which meant they both promptly fell to the ground. Luckily, the mower was the push kind and stopped when he let go of a bar on the handle. "Rex, you're here!"

She threw her arms around his neck and squeezed him tightly to her body. "I thought you were gone, that I'd never see you again!"

"Whoa, Ann! Let me up! If they see me on the ground I'll be in trouble."

"If who sees you, silly? My dad's the king around here now. Nobody can punish you." She got off of him anyway and sat up on the grass. "Isn't it glorious? Look at all of these flowers."

"Yeah, it's great, Ann. I guess your dad is the new lord and master then?" He didn't look as pleased as she'd hoped he'd be, but she brushed it off.

"The overlords decided that since he was a lawyer in the past, he had the most knowledge to get the job done." She brushed back her hair and looked at him. "So, what have you been assigned to do?"

"This, Ann. I'm a wolf. This is what we're used for." He got back up, brushed off his pants, and went back to mowing, while Ann sat still, stunned all over again.

11

"What do you mean, you're all servants?" John asked later that evening, the Wolfson family now in the grand living room with the Adamses.

"We're basically slaves, John," Stephan said, his eyes down on the tiled floor. "Wolves are seen as damaged goods. Our DNA is not to mingle with non-wolves. If we try to marry, mate with, or create a child with a human, for lack of a better term, we'll be sent to a firing squad."

Ann looked over the Wolfson family. They didn't look as clean as the Adamses did, their arms still had fine hair on them, which meant they hadn't had that laser treatment thing, and they still had that hunted look to them that the entire group had the last week before they were captured. She didn't like this one bit.

"But you're no different to us, you just…" Her words failed, and she awkwardly came to a stop. She thought harder for a moment and carried on, "it's not like you're killers, or felons, you haven't committed a crime!"

"Oh no, and it's a good thing your dad dragged us down to that hellhole of his too. All wolves that have killed humans, no matter if they were in their wolf form, especially if they were in their wolf form, are put to death immediately. They have some kind of brain scanner that finds out what you've done. I didn't understand it, but it worked. There was a group in with us, that told us all about what they'd done while the world was ice." Rex shuddered to a stop.

"They'd become cannibals," Amanda said softly. "And seemed very proud of it, too."

The Adamses all stared at her before she carried on. "I don't like it, Stephan doesn't like it, but we have to do what we have to do. Rex, you'll get used to it, I hope." She touched her son's hand, but he pulled away.

"I don't want to be anybody's servant. Especially that shit, mowing grass in this heat." Rex looked as if he might spit on the floor, but then sat back.

"So, you were assigned to us?" Mary asked. The Wolfsons all nodded, and Mary did the same. "Good, at least we'll treat you like family. John, can't you do something about this?"

Her father had been at the writing desk in the

corner, his gaze concentrated on the file he'd been given. "No, it doesn't seem so."

He looked up, his eyes tired and red, before he came to sit with Ann and Mary on the couch.

"The overlords, as they keep calling themselves, have declared you're all servants. It doesn't matter if you killed or not, you're all considered, well," her father paused and swallowed before he continued, "well, subhuman."

"I am not!" Rex shot up from his seat. "I was the captain of the softball team, and on my way to being captain on the football team. I was not some…"

"Shut up, Rex." Stephan yanked his son back down to the couch as if he was still a child and not a full-grown man.

Ann looked away, embarrassed. But she wasn't sure if her embarrassment was for Rex, or what his father had done. A prickle of doubt edged at her love for Rex, and memories tried to come back. She stood up and paced over to the glass wall to stare out at the ocean in the distance. It was clear and as blue as pictures she'd seen of the Bahamas long ago. It hadn't been that *way before*.

"It doesn't matter. I'm still going to marry you, Rex. It doesn't mean anything to me."

"Uh, you can't sweetheart," John said from his side of the couch. "It's forbidden, remember?"

"Then we just won't tell them, right, Rex?" She looked at him, but he wouldn't look at her. She frowned, why wouldn't he look at her?

Okay, so he'd never actually said he wanted to marry her. That wasn't a problem, though, was it? He hadn't said he didn't want to marry her either, so she was running with the assumption that he would and did want to marry her. "Rex?"

"Whatever, Ann. I'm going back to our quarters." Rex left the room without another word. Ann stared after him, but she didn't protest. The way he'd said quarters had silenced her. They were really servants, with their own living area. Quarters, as he'd said.

"I'm sorry, Ann. Rex is taking this hard," Amanda said, her face sympathetic.

"Oh, of course! I don't blame him, at all. It's not like you have a choice in this. It's a new world, I don't under-stand why we have to have these kinds of prejudices still." She inhaled deeply and let it out. "Well, if we can't marry, we'll just have to do the best we can. Maybe we can have a party of some kind..."

"Ann, I don't think you're thinking this through," Stephan started but Ann shook her head.

"I am. We can't have babies, we can't get married, fine. I'll live here, and he can live with you all, and we won't have babies. That doesn't mean we can't still be together."

"It does, Ann," her father said with a heavy sigh. "But I know saying no will only make things worse, so do what you feel is right."

"I will." She lifted her chin, proud of the way she had stood up for herself and Rex. "They can't control every moment of our days. I won't let them."

ANN LEARNED how true those words were over the next month. They saw very little of the alien invaders, their overlords, over the days that passed. One delivered some sort of hovercraft to Ann's father as transport. The vehicles left on Earth consumed far too much fuel, inefficiently, and only a few were ever used. Those were being phased out as workers built more of the transporters the aliens used.

It was little more than a circular bottom, with a glass top that came down, something straight up out of the old Jetsons cartoons she'd watched with her dad when she was a kid. It didn't make the noise that the crafts did in the cartoon, it was almost too quiet, in fact. A lever controlled which direction the craft moved in, and Ann soon learned to drive it as she squired her father around town.

Rex might hate his time as a gardener, but she often assured him it was better than being a glorified secretary/driver. She'd sit for hours sometimes, with very little to do. There weren't a lot of people for her father to rule over yet, but he often met with other leaders to discuss policies they'd planned to put in place in this brand-new world.

"Ann, I have something for you to do this evening. You'll need to take Rex. I left some books at the bunker, some that we need here now. I want you to get them back for me. That alright?"

"Of course, Dad." It would be a moment to be alone with Rex. Maybe they could have a romantic picnic, and he'd hold her hand.

Not like that brute in her dreams, she thought as her father went into the building. She'd taken up reading regency romances, about the only kind of books still left in the library in town, while she waited for her dad to finish with his work. She'd learned the word brute from those books and used it now when she thought about the man in her dreams.

She'd decided there must be something wrong with her, to keep dreaming about a fictional man, and about those kinds of things. She blushed as the sun rose higher overhead. She could blame it on the heat coming through the clear glass, but she knew it was the things he did. The things he said.

She'd dreamed only a few short hours ago about the man in her bedroom.

"Nice choice. I thought you'd choose the white one." She'd scrambled out of the bed, in her dream, to demand he leave, but he only smiled at her.

"I'd have chosen this room too. It holds so much naughty promise, with all of that red. Kind of like your cheeks." His fingers had brushed against her red skin there, and she'd frozen. She wanted him so much but hated that she did.

No, it was better not to think about it, she thought and picked up the latest romance novel she'd found in her wanderings. She couldn't concentrate though. Even though she didn't often get to wander around the city being reborn in front of her eyes, she still had more freedom than the wolves did. They weren't allowed to be out without a human by their side.

The overlords feared the wolves would shift, without warning, and start killing pure-blood humans. As if they didn't know that wolves had cycles, and known dates when they would change. The aliens knew far more about both species now than anyone in history ever had. Their technologies were far more advanced, in all ways, and Ann felt that the measure was only in place to keep the wolves submissive, in invisible chains. She didn't like it, not one bit.

There was little she could do about it, though. At least her parents understood and tried to help her out. She still had to put him off about the whole sex thing, she wanted to wait until she had that one special night, a romantic night filled with love and the promise of a future. She could deal with it, though, if it meant she was Rex's at the end of it all. She could wait and put up with his growing frustration with her.

She hadn't told her mom that he still pestered her for sex. She was a grown woman, she'd decided. She needed to handle this on her own. They had the night all planned out. Well, she did. Rex insisted she do it all because it was her dream night. He said he didn't want to spoil any of it with his interference.

The poor man was too tired, she thought, so she didn't blame him for getting out of doing anything about their day. They couldn't have a wedding, but her father could give her away to him, and she would wear a pretty dress, and that would be enough. That's what she told herself anyway.

She sighed and put the book down when she saw her father come out of the courthouse in front of her. She turned the transporter on and opened the hatch to let him in.

"There may not be much shade in these things," he complained as he climbed in, "but at least they're cooler than the air outside."

"Yes, we can shrivel up in the UV rays in comfort." She pushed the lever that would move them forward and took her father home in quiet.

The aliens were supposed to send out a new line of upper shields, ones that would go as dark as sunglasses during the day, but go clear at night. Ann couldn't wait for those, she decided as she pulled into the driveway of their home. A home she still hadn't become accustomed to.

It was far too big for them, and now that she knew she wouldn't be allowed to have Rex's children, well, there was no hope of filling the rooms up. That made her sad, but it was worth it to have Rex as her lover for the rest of her life. Maybe she could adopt a child, in the future, when more children came into the world. Like little Ricardo, that they'd left behind all those weeks ago.

She still wondered if they were out there. Maybe she'd check on them this evening, when they went back to the bunker. She went to the kitchen and had Amelia, their cook, prepare a meal that was mostly vegetarian. There was little meat to be had, although the overlords were working to restore animal, insect, and plant life. Fish were plentiful, but that was about all. She didn't want to take fish on a picnic, so Amelia prepared dishes that would keep in the transporter's refrigerator.

At 5 pm, an hour after Rex was supposed to finish for the day, Ann was in the transporter, candles, wine glasses, a couple of blankets, and the food tucked away. Rex came, grim as always, but with a slight smile for his soon to be 'wife'.

"At least we get some time alone together. We can talk for ages." Ann smiled broadly and pressed the button to close the glass. "Ready?"

"Yeah, I guess," he said and settled into the backseat. It was a wide couch that followed the shape of the vehicle.

"I thought you'd sit up here with me."

"I'm beat, Ann. Let me just rest for a while. I mowed two acres of grass today, with a push mower." Rex threw his arm over his eyes, and Ann looked away, her face a mask of hurt.

He was right, though, she thought as the transporter, a much faster vehicle than a car, pulled away. For a moment, she thought about trying to run away, thought about taking the vehicle and driving up to Canada. Or over to Alaska and then to Russia. Were the aliens over there?

She didn't know how far they'd gotten; she just knew that every few days, more people would be released into the new zones set up around the city. She still thought of them as kingdoms sometimes, but now, she could see they more resembled zones. Especially when they were up high like this.

When she neared the place where she knew the sisters, May and Kay, had lived, she slowed down. She was going to stop, but the fact that the building had burned down told her there was little point in stopping.

All that was left of the place was ash. The aliens or someone else, she wondered. A tear slid down her cheek, and she brushed it away. She'd have her father check, find out what happened to them, she decided, and carried on.

It wasn't hard work to fly the things, but it would tire out your hand. She switched her hands constantly, to keep from getting cramps. Soon enough, they were over the area where the bunker was. Ann landed the craft but didn't wake Rex up. He needed to sleep, she decided. She went down, got the books she needed, and was headed to a spot where she knew they could see the waters from the ocean, without being too near the city.

"Later, Ann. Wake me up later," Rex rumbled when she tried to wake him up.

"But Rex, I have a picnic…"

"Leave me alone, Ann!" he roared and sat up to glare at her with angry, red eyes. "Fuck!"

Ann glared back at him as he went back down on the couch, her eyes full of angry tears. She wiped them away and went back to her driver's seat. She knew he was tired, she knew that, but did that give him the right to talk to her like that?

She felt the thick tang of tears in her mouth, and that only made her angrier. She was such a ninny; he was only tired. That didn't mean it didn't hurt, though.

12

____

Ann sat at a cheap, pine kitchen table in the expansive kitchen, a fire going in the fireplace, just because her mother liked the look of it. The lights had been dimmed, and the women worked in a soft glow. It reminded them all of the bunker and more peaceful times.

She knew it was odd to think of those years in the bunker as peaceful, but they were. Her days had been filled with lessons from one parent or another the first few years, and then she'd continued her studies on her own. She'd learned about so many different things from the textbooks down there, and she'd thought the enclosed space was a cocoon, a place of peace that she missed now.

Amelia had the night off, and rather than have another woman come in to cook, Mary always invited the Wolfsons over and the three women would all work together to prepare the meal. Ann was pulling the green cover and silk from ears of corn, shelling peas, and peeling carrots to go with the meal. They'd all sit in here, around the fire, and eat, each with a glass of wine at hand.

It was the only time the Wolfsons felt like real people again. Amanda, Stephan, and Rex would be released from the duties given to them by the butler, who was the head of the servants at the house, and they'd have the night to themselves. Tonight, the men were outside grilling fish, while the women prepared a soup and some pasta to go with it.

"I've noticed something," Amanda said, unafraid to speak to her new 'mistress', without anyone else around. If someone was, Amanda would bow her head, subservient in her bland, blue uniform dress that looked as if it had escaped some women's prison back in the 1960s and had taken on new life in the present.

"What's that?" Mary asked, her eyes on the pasta she'd had resting for hours now.

"Well," Amanda paused as she stirred the base for the soup Ann had peeled the carrots for. "There are no alien females."

"What?" Mary asked and stopped rolling the pasta dough out. "What do you mean?"

Ann's ears perked and she listened quietly, as she

always had. The two women would often forget, as they counted out MREs and rationed out hot water, that Ann was in the room. That, or they thought she wouldn't understand what they were discussing, because it never seemed to occur to them that she could hear them. So, she'd often stayed quiet, listened, and learned far more than they'd ever tell her, even now, when she was an adult.

She sipped at the Muscadine wine the aliens had found and appreciated the fact that age limits for wine consumption no longer existed. She loved the stuff.

"Well, I've only seen males, and they call themselves overlords. Women wouldn't be called that, would they? I mean, they wouldn't be called overladies, that would just be absurd, but that's a clue too, isn't it? I don't think..." Amanda paused, looked around, and then whispered, but loud enough that Ann could hear. "I don't think they have any females with them."

Ann sat up, her eyes somewhere around the ceiling as she thought back over the last few weeks. She had not seen any female aliens. Ever. Oh, that was worrying.

"That one, when we were first taken," Mary said nervously and glanced over at Ann. "The one that said I could still make babies."

"Mom, now don't panic!" Ann said in a warning voice and stood to take her mothers arms in her hands. "Maybe they aren't allowed to leave the ship. Maybe they are on their way, you'll see. There's nothing to panic about. They wouldn't put us in this nice house, give us nice food, and tasks to complete if they just wanted to use us as baby-making machines."

Ann knew that's exactly where her mother's mind had gone. She remembered the moment her mom had mentioned. She'd thought the remark odd, but obviously it had unsettled her mother a great deal. She knew her mother didn't plan to have any more children. She was young enough to still have one though, if she wanted to.

"I don't want more children... I don't want... that either." Mary waved her hand in the air, but they all knew what she meant. Being forced to mate with an alien.

"I can't have anymore. I tried after Rex, I wanted a girl. Desperately. We tried, and then we tried IVF. We finally gave up and decided we were destined to have one. I doubt they'd want me, even if that was their plan. I think..." Amanda had also tried to comfort Mary with a hand on her arm. She moved away, though, and went back to stirring the pot of soup broth.

"You think what, Amanda?" Ann asked and stepped closer to the other woman.

"I think they'll want the young women like you, Ann." She turned back to them, her hands out in front of her as if to hold off questions. "I've heard things, from some of the wolves that go to other houses sometimes. Things I don't want to repeat, but this, I think you both should know."

"Tell us, Amanda! For fuck's sake, tell us!" Mary was on the verge of hysteria, and Ann pulled her mother into her arms.

"I've heard they're taking the younger women for breeding programs with the aliens. That's why they want only pure-bloods. We wolves can't mate with the aliens. They're almost human, but not exactly. And the wolf DNA is too different. The babies would be mutated, deformed, so we've been cast down as slaves."

She paused, took a deep breath and then spoke again. "There's also word that all of us women will be forced to reproduce with our mates, if we have one. Those who don't will be part of the alien breeding program."

Ann swayed on her feet but stood tall for her mother's sake. "They can't force us to have sex with those men."

"It won't be that way. They'll use something like IVF, from what I've heard. They're doing it already in the first cities they cleared."

"Fuck!" Mary exclaimed and went to sit at the table. "Ann? What about Ann? I'll have another baby with John if I have to, but she shouldn't be forced to do… any of that."

"I'm still a virgin," Ann said softly and took a seat

beside her mother. "It would be funny if it wasn't so frightening."

"A virgin birth…" Amanda sighed and sat down too. "We can move up your date with Rex if you want?"

"I think that might be best, don't you?" She didn't really want to, she didn't know what to do, in reality, but it was something to focus on. "I'll go into the dress stores tomorrow, see what I can find."

It wouldn't be a real wedding, but close enough for Ann. She took a deep breath and tried not to panic. "We don't even know if it's true; it could just be a rumor."

The other women nodded and went back to their tasks.

"I guess we need to repopulate the world somehow," Mary said and got back up to finish cooking. It wasn't like preparing MREs. They'd always made that last as long as they could, to pretend they'd done something akin to cooking, but this took actual thinking and planning, so they all followed Mary's lead.

"I can't believe it's real," Amanda said. But then she looked at Mary with something like hope. "I always did want a daughter though. Someone sweet and loving, like Ann."

"Aw, thanks," Ann said and smiled, pleased for a moment.

"If they can give me another baby, I don't think I'd complain. As long as it's Stephan's baby, of course.

Maybe they have some alien voodoo that can fix whatever's broken in me."

"I hope they do, Amanda. I'm not sure… I hadn't planned on…" but Ann could see the speculation in her mother's eye.

Ann had always wanted a baby brother or sister. It seemed her mother was thinking about it now. They did have a lot of rooms to fill, after all. Ann looked away with a smile, but it faded. Would she be forced to carry some unknown alien's baby?

For some reason, the man in her dreams came to mind. As always, she tried to push thoughts of him away, but he was always there, always ready to ruin her day with some pleasurable remnant of her dreams. He was a fine specimen of what a man should be, there was no doubt of that. Healthy, fit, and as handsome as any actor she'd ever seen, and she'd seen a few when she visited her father's office. He would make pretty babies. If he didn't have orange eyes.

They were the color of a tiger's orange stripes, deep and full of fire. She thought the color would be unnerving in a child. She sometimes found light blue or gray eyes unsettling and wondered if the light hurt their eyes, but she tried to tell herself that was silly. She was even more silly to consider whether a dream lover could give her a child.

What the hell is wrong with me, she wondered, and not for the first time.

Her mother and Amanda had gone back to cooking, so she did the same. An hour later, the men came in with plates full of grilled fish, the pasta was cooked, the soup puréed and the corn ready to drown in… margarine.

Ann frowned at the tub on the plate. They could clear away ice, a bad atmosphere, and bring life back to the planet, but margarine was the best they could produce in the way of butter-like substances. With a sigh, she spread some of the stuff on her corn and doused it in salt.

"You're going to wish you hadn't used that much salt when you're older, dear," her father warned her, as he always did.

"I can't help it. I think it was all of those MREs over the years. They must have been full of salt. The food just doesn't taste as good without a ton of salt on it."

"You could be right, although most of them were dehydrated and low in sodium. Not all of them were, though." John plucked a speckle of fish onto his fork and went back to eating.

After dinner, Ann and Rex washed dishes. He was already eyeing the door, ready to go to bed, but she asked him to stay and talk with her at the table once they'd put the last dish away.

"How are you doing?" Ann asked, her hand on his.

He ignored her hand, but she could see he was thinking. Lost in thought.

"I've met some other wolves our age." He didn't look at her, he just stared into the night beyond the large window beside the door that led out to the back. "There's talk of… revolution."

"Revolution, Rex? Against who? You can't mean the overlords. They would defeat any movement in a minute." They'd all seen the aliens' might, their ability to squash insurrection, of any kind. They'd captured Ann's group easily enough, after all.

"But there might be a way. I'm meeting them later. I'll find out more then."

"Rex," she drew out his name teasingly, but with a smile. "Come on now, you know you can't defeat them, right?"

"But we can, Ann! We might even be able to escape them. I'll find out more tonight, and then you'll see. You'll believe me." He pulled away from her hand, stung by her disbelief. "I can't believe you want to give up so easily to them."

"I don't, Rex. We can't marry or have children because of them. I want them to go back where they came from and leave us alone." She didn't mention what his mother had revealed earlier. He was already riled up enough as it was. She placed her hand over his heart and looked into his eyes, so full of hurt and anger. "I can't fight them, not right now anyway."

"You mean you don't want to. And why should you?" He stood up to pace around the kitchen. "You get to live in this. I'm your servant! If anything, it should be the other way around!"

After he said it, he looked around, as if James might be just around the corner. When he didn't see anyone, he carried on.

"You're nothing but a helpless woman, and you're only human. We wolves are far stronger, much hardier than you pure-bloods. You're weak and should be the ones waiting on us hand and foot!"

The last part was sneered, and Ann stared at Rex, truly stunned at the venom in his voice. "Rex, you don't mean that?"

Fear suddenly swept over his face, and he turned away to hide whatever else he might feel from her. "You're right, of course. That was silly of me. I just... I got carried away. I'm sorry, Ann."

The sudden change in Rex surprised her and she blinked at him. What had just happened? Then it dawned on her and her eyes went round. She had some power, then. She hadn't realized it, but she did. He was afraid he'd stepped over the line and she'd report him to the aliens. He wasn't sure he could trust her, which hurt, but he was also afraid of the power she had. She wasn't sure she disliked that, though she knew she should.

"It's alright, Rex. Just be careful, will you?" She looked at him, frustrated that he'd been so stupid. "You never know who's listening, anyway." She made a motion with her eyes and eyebrows to draw his gaze to the button for calling servants. She always wondered if that button could see or hear them. She didn't trust it much, and she'd now had two conversations today that could get them all in trouble. All in view of that button.

"You're right. Sorry about that. Um, I have to go. Catch you later, okay?"

She waved goodbye to him but wondered what kind of trouble he was about to cause them all and if she should talk to her father about it. With a sigh, she went to bed instead. Not that she'd find any peace in her dreams, but she would find pleasure. That was something in this odd world she lived in.

13

—————

*A*nn thought about her friends, Elizabeth and Maria, for the first time in many years that evening. They'd all been typical teenage girls, laughing and giggling over anything and everything. They'd all been the same age, but Elizabeth had been the smallest, pale, petite and blond. Maria had the darker skin of her mother, an immigrant from Honduras, the dark eyes, and all of that enviable black hair.

They'd all been so different from each other, but the moment they met in kindergarten, they'd been friends. That friendship had lasted through the years of their education, and the changes that puberty had wrought in them. For Ann, that meant getting her period and growing boobs before the other two. They'd been so jealous but pleased for Ann. They'd soon followed though, and they all headed straight into maturity with glee.

They'd known everything about each other. Maria's fascination with another girl at their school, Elizabeth's preoccupation with getting the best grades out of anyone else in their grade, and Ann's obsession with Rex. They'd both thought Rex was a douche, but Ann loved him, and she'd ignored their dislike.

What would they say now, she wondered, alone in her room? Would they tell her to run from the aliens, to enlist Rex's help and escape? Or would they tell her to run from Rex? That was probably what they would tell her, but they didn't know Rex like she did, they didn't see the man he could be, if he'd just try a little bit harder.

She braided her hair for the tenth time that day and stared at herself in the mirror. She wasn't ugly. Some might even say she was pretty. Her nose was small and suited her face, her parents had spent a fortune on braces for her when she was 13, and she now had straight, white teeth. Her skin was clear, and her eyes were a pleasant shade of brown.

Her body had filled out as she matured, and she now had the hips that went with her breasts, and a slim waist, mainly a gift of nature. She'd kept up the walking though, even now that they were in a safe place with no need to stay fit. She liked walking in the garden, learning about the flowers that were now theirs. She had always been inquisitive, and while she might not have had the grades that Elizabeth had maintained, she was a good student, with a sharp mind.

Or so her father had always told her.

She'd pushed memories of her friends away, along with the family that she might have lost. Her mother had a brother somewhere up in West Virginia, and her dad had a sister that lived in Oklahoma. They hadn't heard anything about any of them, friends or family, and didn't have much hope that they ever would.

The aliens hadn't put out a list of survivors, but maybe they should. Ann wrote a note to herself to ask her father about that and went to climb into her bed. She'd showered, put on a pair of black silk pajamas, and was ready for bed. She picked up the book she had, an old copy of something by Anne Rice; Ann couldn't tell what the book was because the paperback cover and the first few pages were missing. She didn't care, she just needed to escape, and the tale of witches and ancient beings fascinated her.

The hours passed, and Ann turned off the overhead light and turned on her bedside lamp. She was so close to sleep, but she wanted to finish one more chapter. She didn't realize she'd closed her eyes and that the book had fallen from her fingers until a crash of sound came from the area around her bedroom.

What was that?

She got out of bed, opened the doors, and saw a dozen pebbles on the ground. Was it Rex? Was he trying to get her attention?

She went to the edge of her small balcony and looked over.

"Ann, come down! Hurry! We need to talk!" he said in a very loud whisper, his face animated with urgency.

"Rex? Fine! I'll be down in a minute." She ran back into her room, slipped on a pair of flip flops and a robe, and quietly made her way down to one of the back-doors. There were several at the back of the house.

"Ann, come on, follow me." Rex grabbed her hand the second she closed the door and ran down to the disguised tool shed where most of the tools he used were kept. There wasn't anyone else there at this time of night, she knew, and smiled. He wanted to have some time alone with her.

A pleased glow of heat spread in her chest, and she went to sit down on a plastic chair in the corner of the small shed. "What's going on?"

"I met with the group, Ann. It's going to happen; the revolution is real!" He all but danced with joy, and Ann felt the glow turn cold.

She'd hoped he'd wanted to talk to her about their relationship, about how much he loved her. He hadn't said it yet, but surely, he must love her? The way he wanted to kiss her all the time, and all of that other stuff? That was love, wasn't it? Yet, here he was, talking about some stupid revolution that had no hope of defeating the enemy they'd chosen.

"Rex! Don't be silly! The revolution can't win. Why waste your time?" She saw the way his face changed, from overjoyed glee to cold anger, and decided to change tactics. "Look, I know you hate being a servant, but trying to cause a war isn't the way. You have to change their minds, not try to destroy them. We have so much to learn from the aliens, look at their technology. Why do you want to fight that? Embrace it, and then change the rules with them, convince them to do it. You can't win a war against them."

"I should have known you'd take their side. You're going to become their whore, their baby factory, and still have a nice life. Not like Mom, who has to work for you and your sniveling family for nothing. Some food, clothing, and shelter. What the fuck kind of life is that?"

"Rex! Don't be cruel! I know why you want to do this, I understand that, but war isn't the way. And no," Ann stood up from her seat to look into his eyes. To her surprise, he actually backed up as she stalked towards him. "I don't want to be some baby-making breeder for alien babies, or for anyone for that matter. I don't even want that stupid house, or the luxuries we've been given. I'd give anything to be back in the bunker, where it was just my family and yours, making our own rules and plans for the future."

He was against a wall now, his back pressed into a pair of garden shears. "You wouldn't give up that room and the pool, all those books you're always reading. You like this new world, the aliens. You don't have to live this new life like I do."

"I know I don't, that's why I try to include you in the things I can do. When I ask James to send you to me to clear the vines around my balcony, I'm really asking to have time with you, to sit there and enjoy it together. When I tell James the grass around the pool needs cutting, I'm giving you time to join me there. Can't you see, you silly man? I'm not rubbing your nose in my new luxuries, I'm trying to include you. Which means I'm subverting the aliens."

He just watched her, his eyes narrowed, but he wasn't as tense as he'd been earlier.

"Most of all, I plan to spend the rest of my life with you. We're planning a ceremony to declare that intention before our parents and each other. Okay, so it's not the wedding I would have liked to plan, but it's close enough. How much more do I need to prove myself to you?"

Rex relaxed for the first time in a long time and slid down to the floor. His plain jeans and denim short-sleeved shirt were stained with oil and paint, but all of his clothes were now.

"I don't want you to prove yourself, I…" he stopped and looked away, anger still in his eyes. He had more to say, Ann could see it, but he kept it bottled inside, the same as always. "I just want to be equals again."

"That's rich coming from you," she said quickly and then slapped her hands over her mouth. Her eyes were wide with mortification and she knew she shouldn't have said it.

"What's that supposed to mean?"

In for a penny, in for a pound, she thought as she stared down at him from the chair she'd reclaimed. She had a lot of her own hurt and anger bottled up inside, maybe now was the time to clear the air, when he was actually listening to her for a change.

"You always acted so high and mighty, Rex. Like you were king of the world, not just the school. That school must have seen dozens of boys like you in its time. But even in the bunker, you were too good to do most of the chores that needed to be done. It was our own fault, we coddled you and left you to wallow in your misery, because you were supposed to be a star…"

"Really?" His tone told her she'd gone way too far, but she wasn't about to back down now.

"Really." She gave a quick shake of her head to emphasize her point. "And look at you now. Do you think it would be any different if the aliens hadn't made you a servant? You'd work your ass off every day, and for what? The same things you have now. Only, you'd get to make a choice about which slave-wage job you'd be performing."

"You sure seem to be certain about that," he said softly, and she knew she should be more careful, but something deep inside drove her to empty out every last thing she'd squirreled away. Every argument, every hurt he'd given her, no matter how petty, wanted to come out of her now.

"I am certain, Rex. This new world is no different from the old world in many respects. Yes, there are aliens now, and some super-weird technology, but do you think life is really any different? My dad was a lawyer before all of this, and he's not a wolf, so he's in charge. He wasn't given that designation before, but he was one of those people that was in charge, even back then. He made sure the law was upheld, and that people didn't get shafted. He worked and did well at his job. He has skills; what do you have? No more than me, the ability to do as we're told by our parents, or those in charge of us, and to get on with life the best we can."

He only glared at *her, but* then, there wasn't much he could argue against. He was a wolf, fate had decreed that to be the case, and the same as any other culture that had been subjugated in American history, he couldn't complain about it much. It wouldn't do him any good. The aliens now had far more power than any senator, governor, or president could have ever hoped to have. They even had more power than the military had before the end came.

"You want to take part in some revolution, like every other silly boy in history has done, certain that his cause is just. But what are you really going to accomplish with that revolution, Rex? Are you going to get yourself killed? Your parents maybe? Me? Would you even care if the rest of us died, as long as you finally, finally, got to have your mega-sized temper tantrum at the fate you were handed?"

"Ann…" he started to say but looked away.

She'd expected him to explode, to scream at her. Instead, he just… looked away. But he didn't stay quiet, not for long.

"When you're being controlled by an alien, Ann, when you spend the rest of your life pregnant for one of them, you'll wish there'd been a revolution. You're a woman anyway. You're too stupid to know what's good for you." He flicked a piece of rubber he'd been twisting around in his hand to the floor and stood up. "I'll save you, even if you don't want to be saved, Ann. It's my job."

With that, he walked away. His last statement made it clear that he still thought she needed to be saved. She just didn't know what he wanted to save her from. Boys and their stupid need to nobly save women. It was something she hated about those regency romances and was why she'd picked up that other book. The women always needed to be saved. She loved the stories, of course, but why couldn't a woman save herself?

This was a new world, women had options now, they weren't all dependent on men to come along on a white horse and sweep them away. Some, most, had the ability to change their lives without a man in modern times. Well, maybe not so much now, but before.

Which made her stop. She'd been living in her own dream world, hadn't she? She hadn't seen any women in positions of power here. Only men were in the places where leadership took place. Maybe there'd been no female lawyers left after the last few years?

But what about women like Amanda? She'd been a teacher, a really good one. Yet, she was little more than her mother's cook now, and a cleaner the rest of the time. And her mother was just the wife of a leader. She had no real role other than that.

Things would change, though, as time went on and more people were found. Ann had to hang on to that hope. Otherwise, maybe she was no better off than those women in the past who'd had to turn to a man for help. And she didn't want that to be the case at all.

14

The ceremony was only a few days away now, and Ann was on the hunt for a dress a few days later. She had been surprised when Rex hadn't called off the ceremony the day after their talk in the shed. She had been afraid that she might have been too frank with him, too blunt, but he'd waved when he'd seen her at the pool.

She'd had to take her father to a meeting with the supreme overlord, and he'd said he might be there for a few hours. This part of the city hadn't been destroyed, and it was full of shops. The kind of shops she needed to find the right dress for her big day. And, even if it wasn't a real wedding, she wanted the right kind of dress.

Once her father left, she turned off their transporter, closed it up, and went out in search of the perfect dress. The first shop had two levels of floor space, and every dress she tried on was beautiful, but the dress would need to be tailored, or it was stained with something, or too old to hold up for long. The dresses might have been kept out of the open elements, but years of constant cold had taken their toll.

She finally got tired of looking, and went to another shop, across the street. This one was only one floor, but she found the dress she wanted, hidden in the back in a box. She'd found the display dress, got the code for it, and had gone back to check, her hopes high. She dug the box with her size out of the stack and opened it.

The dress had been sealed in a bag for at least five years, but it was clean and would serve her purposes. She tried it on and knew with some help to tie the corset back, that the dress would be perfect. She put the dress in a shopping bag, grabbed a few accessories, and a pair of shoes, and headed back to the transporter.

She then went back, found a tuxedo in Rex's size, shirt and shoes to go with it, and a suit for her father and Stephan. Then she found a dress for her mother, in the exact shade of blue to match her eyes, and one in a shimmery copper color for Amanda. The ceremony was to be a very private occasion, between her, Rex and their parents. Nobody else was invited. Later, the servants would have the day off and John had promised a barbecue for them all.

Chickens had been raised from extinction, somehow,

and her father ordered enough to feed them all. It wouldn't be the wedding, or the reception, she'd dreamed about as a teenager, but close enough. Her father would repeat the vows for them, as the highest-ranking person in their district. Later in the evening, Rex and Ann would leave the party to a room Ann had chosen on the other side of the house, well out of anyone's notice.

Not a honeymoon, she knew, but she couldn't ask for much. Not when even sleeping with Rex was forbidden under the laws put in place by the aliens. She'd found rings for them both, a few days before, and now she had the attire that would make the day special. She'd have to take it off almost as soon as she put it on, but it didn't matter. The moments when she did wear it were what mattered.

Her father came bustling out of the office building she'd dropped him in front of and climbed into the transporter. He paused when he saw all of the bags. "Found what you were looking for, my dear?"

He strapped into his seat and didn't look at the bags again. He didn't look at her either. "What's wrong?"

"Nothing, sweetheart. Let's get home." He patted her hand, and then took up his stance as sentry once more.

Ann wasn't sure what exactly was wrong, or how she knew something was wrong. He'd gone in nervous; he always was when he met with the aliens, but he normally came out all smiles. That was probably what tipped her off then, she thought as she turned the transporter on and headed back home. He'd worn a frown when he came out of the building, and his eyes had tracked everything around him. He still did it, as she guided them into the driveway of their home a little while later.

He got out, grabbed the bags, but kept his gaze on the area around him. He didn't seem to relax until they made their way indoors and then he still seemed tense. John normally kept up a steady stream of chatter when he was around her or her mother, but today, he was quiet and strained.

"You're home! Good!" her mother called as she came down the stairs. "What did you find?"

John pecked his wife on the cheek and then left to go up to their bedroom. Ann picked up the bags and headed to the study. "Call Amanda, have her come in too, please."

Her mother used the buzzer on the hallway door and directed James to send Amanda to the large study in there. The women had long ago learned to not be overly modest around each other. Ann stripped off her clothes, down to the underwear she'd found in her drawers upstairs and pulled the dress out of the bag.

"Oh, honey, that ivory color is beautiful." Mary's hand came out and touched the silky soft material of the lace dress, and her voice went quiet. "It's so beautiful."

The material had a shimmery shine to it, but not too much. Ann shook out the lace dress and displayed the handkerchief sleeves and the corset back of the a-line dress with a small train. It was elegant, romantic, and stylish. Everything she wanted to be on her wedding day. Her mother's eyes filled with tears when she slipped into it. Ann turned and her mother did up the buttons and tightened the corset back until the dress fit Ann perfectly.

Ann heard a knock at the door and then Amanda slipped inside. Amanda stopped, stunned at just how innocent and beautiful Ann looked. She said as much as she walked up to the young woman.

"You just… you look so sweet… beautiful and innocent, but sexy too!" Amanda's nose turned red and her eyes started to fill with tears. "Oh no. I don't know why I'm crying. You just look so gorgeous, Ann!"

The three women laughed at each other and then hugged as Ann tried to change the subject. "Look, there are dresses in those two bags, a small flower crown I plan to wear, and shoes and stuff. I think I brought everything we need. The two black bags are the men's suits and Rex's tux."

"I think you cleared the store out, Ann!" Amanda

laughed and pulled out the copper dress Ann chose for her. "Oh my, that is sexy!"

"I thought you'd like it." Ann grinned. Amanda never had been the kind to dress up much, always more concerned with serviceability, rather than glamor. But it was a special moment, she deserved the moment to feel glamorous and beautiful. As did her mother.

Both were still young women, after all, in the grand scheme of things, and had plenty of life left in them. She didn't see why either woman should hide away like matrons now that they'd reached 40. "Go on, try them on!"

"Oh, sorry, I was too busy *looking* at it, Ann. It's beautiful!" Mary quickly dropped the dress, wiggled out of her jeans and silk shirt, and put the dress on. It fit her a little tight in the bust, but it would only draw her father's eyes, Ann decided with a grin.

"You look gorgeous, Mom!"

"Ann, neither one of us can outshine you, honey," Amanda said, her eyes filled with pride as she looked at the young woman.

"Well, you're doing pretty well, lady!" Amanda had slid on the coppery silk, and it encased her skin as though it had been made for her.

They'd have probably carried on wearing the dresses and trying on the things Ann had brought them if someone hadn't started to pound at the front door. They all paused as they heard James open the door. Ann felt the fine hair on her body stand on end and some awareness overcame her.

"Change, hurry!" She helped Amanda get out of the dress and back into her clothes and was handing her mother her pants when the door flew open.

They all yelped in surprise and Mary quickly pulled her pants on. Ann's body went on alert, and she somehow knew who was there. Even before she looked up into a pair of orange eyes, she knew.

"That'll do, Ann. It's a beautiful wedding dress." The alien from her dreams stood in the doorway, as if he'd walked through it a hundred times before and hadn't just shocked her into immobility.

How could he be real? He was just some fantasy her brain had dreamed up, wasn't he? But then, he was right there in the door, as if he owned the place, his gaze a hot wave as he looked her up and down. His eyes said he knew her thoughts, knew her dreams, and couldn't wait to make those dreams reality.

She'd have said he was more handsome in the flesh, that he was a supreme example of masculinity and strength, but she couldn't think. Her tongue was glued to the bottom of her mouth, and she was certain she'd never be able to lock her jaw again, it hung open so long. He was real.

Ann's frozen brain suddenly came back to life. Did

he know her plans with Rex? Did he approve of them? Had her father planned this as a surprise?

"Dad?" she called out and saw her father come to stand behind the man. He wouldn't look at Ann, though, still, and that worried her.

"Yes, Ann?"

"What's going on?"

The man dragged her father into the room, a broad grin on his face. It would have terrified her if she hadn't been so shocked, that menacing grin.

"Well now, you see, I've decided to come out of the clouds, and live down here on Earth with you mortals." The man chuckled as if he'd made a great joke, but everyone just stared at him. Even her mother and Amanda were frozen, Ann noted.

What the hell was going on and why did her father continue to hide behind the man?

"It's been a long time since I've seen a woman as lovely as you, Ann. You'll be the perfect wife, I'm sure."

That made her uneasy and the way her father flinched made it even worse.

"I'm sure you can find a suitable place to live and have all the women you want around you." She wasn't sure what to say to him, but she knew she couldn't look away from him.

She was terrified of him, in the flesh. She'd been afraid of him, in her dreams, but that had been because he made her feel so much. She'd been afraid of herself in those dreams, of the things she wanted, things she wanted from him.

She didn't know if this was some kind of new alien seduction technique, or what, but she knew he was the man that appeared in her dreams every single night now.

"I'm sure I could, but I only want one wife. We aren't doing too well at finding women. It's a shame your race of humans has so little value for female life. I've seen cases where, what are they called these men that spent fortunes on building underground homes?" He snapped his fingers, and the leather gloves that his hands were covered in didn't dare to do anything but snap.

"Preppers?" she asked as she finally took him in. He was dressed in leather, from head to toe, and he must be steaming hot in the California heat. At least the shirt looked like a thin version of the material.

"That's it. Preppers!" He spun his head back to her and she saw his black hair had shimmering brown beads tied through the strands. Beads the color of her eyes. She frowned, apprehension a knot that made her stomach queasy. "Anyway, these preppers, all of them determined to save their women and children, ended up trading their women for food, of all things. Can you imagine? And some, well, some used the women as food. Quite nasty, those fellows."

He wandered as he spoke and took a seat on the couch that she'd covered with wedding finery. "Your race of humans, Ann, they aren't to be noted for their compassion, are they?"

"My father and Stephan kept us alive, not all of the humans here are bad, you know. And Stephan's a wolf too, but they still did their best to keep us safe."

"Ah, but there's the problem, Ann. Your father should have thrown those dangerous elements out into the cold. The wolves were far more hearty than you pure-bloods. They could have survived out in the cold."

"But they might have been forced to kill and you kill all the wolves that killed humans," she protested, her chin up in defense and defiance.

"We'll have to discuss the wolves another time, Ann. We have other matters to sort out now."

"And what might those matters be?" She'd started to relax a little, now that he wasn't standing up, so tall and looming over them.

"Surely your father has told you the good news, Ann." He looked up at her father and then back to her. "That's why you have the dress on, right? You know we're going to be married."

"What?" Ann screamed the word, and her eyes went to her father. He looked as if he wanted to crawl into a hole and die, he looked so miserable.

"Yes, my dear. I'm Rager. The man you will soon call

husband." He looked at the other women, who'd all kind of whimpered at the news. "You should be happy, my dear. I'm the supreme commander, the Overlord of the overlords. You're about to marry a very powerful man. But don't worry, I'm repairing a house not far from here, so you can visit your parents when you like."

Married? To an alien? But that meant they didn't plan to leave, that they were colonizing Earth and didn't plan to go. And she was supposed to just marry one of them? Even if he was the man from her dreams, she didn't know him, didn't like what he made her feel in those dreams. Well, the pleasure part was nice, but she never wanted to feel that. Even in her dreams, her brain thought of Rex, and how she was betraying him with this man.

This man whose name was Rager. That couldn't be a good sign either.

"Cat got your tongue?" he asked and then laughed. It was a booming sound that filled the room, until Ann thought the house might very well shake down around them all. "No matter, you'll soon become accustomed to the idea."

"Dad, you have to stop this. He can't be serious! I'm not marrying an alien!" Ann said as soon as the man left, all of the women still too stunned to offer any kind of refreshment to the supreme commander of them all. She paced in front of him, where he still sat, merged with the couch to all appearances.

"He's very serious, Ann. So serious, he'll kill us all if you refuse or try to run away." John's words were little more than a whisper by the time he finished.

"What?" She sat back down on the couch, her pacing at an end at that news.

"If you don't agree, every man and woman in this district will die. I tried to remind him that he needed all of us, and that there were other women, some being found every day, but he wants you. And insisted that you were the only one he wanted." He was too ashamed to look at her.

So, she didn't need to be saved by a marriage to a man, her brain stupidly thought, she needed to save her district by marrying the man. Her parents, the Wolfsons, all the other families that worked at their place, and lived in the surrounding area, they would all die, if she chose to be obstinate or refused to marry the man. Alien.

"Damn, Dad." She took his hand and squeezed his fingers; she knew it wasn't his fault and couldn't be mad at him.

"I'm sorry, honey, I tried to change his mind, I really did."

"You didn't try hard enough!" Mary cried and threw her hands out in front of her body. "Look at all of this stuff, it's for her wedding to Rex! Not some crazy, giant alien!"

"Mom, Dad can't do anything about it. And neither can we." She'd given up already. There was no way around this. None at all.

"I'll tell Rex, Ann. It would be better coming from me. You know how he's been lately," Amanda sighed as she let the dress slide from her fingers and back into the bag.

Like all of her dreams, suddenly useless and unnecessary, she thought as she watched Amanda put the dress away. I won't need them anymore now. I've got to go off and marry this alien. Sure, he was a great lover in her dreams, but pleasure wasn't always the best thing to build a marriage on. There was no trust, no loyalty, and no friendship. They were strangers, and more than that they were two different races of human.

He'd said it more than once, your race of humans. As if they weren't the same. She had to guess that was what he meant. Just like Neanderthals were a separate species, maybe she was different from the aliens. She didn't know and couldn't figure out what it all meant, other than the fact that it meant her life was over.

She didn't care about his power, or who he was, he wasn't Rex, and that's what she cared about. So, Rex was an asshole a lot of the time, he'd calm down once she showed him what it was like to be loved by a woman. He'd come to see that women weren't useless. Or he would have.

"I'm going to check on dinner," she said and left the grown-ups alone in the room. She wanted to scream, to cry, to beat her hands against the walls and refuse it all. But there were so many lives on the line. That brought calmness to her like nothing else could.

She could marry Rex, in a fake little sham of a marriage, or she could marry this alien. One wedding could bring about her own death, and that of Rex and any children they might accidentally have and kill off an entire district. Or she could marry the alien and save them all some grief. She didn't want to, the thought of it made her skin crawl, but she would do what she had to do.

If that meant throwing away the only real hopes she'd had in life, then so be it. But she'd make sure her family, her district, received the fruits of that sacrifice. She would make him pay, every single day that she was his prisoner wife, one way or another.

"Amelia, what's for dinner?" she called out as she came into the kitchen. Amanda went out to the back door and her parents had gone up to their room.

"Chicken and dumplings, Ann. Something your mom asked for."

"She's always cold in this house. It's the air conditioning. When I was little, she'd make that on rainy days, in the summer, because we'd all be so cold in the house, but if we turned off the air it would be too hot. She'd make it in the wintertime, too, but it was always nicest in the summer like that."

"It sounds like a good memory." Amelia, a wolf that had survived in a bunker somewhere in Colorado, was on her own.

She didn't *talk* about her past or her family, but she enjoyed hearing Ann's stories.

"It is. We only had MREs down in the bunker, but she'd tell me to pretend the chicken stew dinners were chicken and dumplings when we found new boxes of them." That didn't happen often; chicken hadn't seemed to be high on the list of things to stick in an MRE, but they'd all enjoyed them when they found them.

"I had cans and cans of food. Took me years to get through them," Amelia said softly. "And then I started on the MREs, that's when I started to wonder if it was worth living, if that was my future."

Ann didn't say anything, she just let the woman speak. She'd mentioned her past so little that Ann wanted to hear more. She wanted to know the woman's story. A thought occurred to her then. Maybe they should write these stories of survival down, just in case there was a future generation.

"I'd collect water from this stream that melted into the bunker my grandpa had dug during the cold war. It kept the place dry and gave me water, so I didn't complain about it. Probably didn't do me any favors, that water, but I'm still here so it couldn't have been too bad."

Ann's family had so much water they thought they'd never use it. Bottles of all sizes, barrels, all sorts, stored water down in the bunker. It had kept them alive and was clean. They hadn't had to worry about that at all.

"It doesn't sound too bad," Ann said softly and sat down at the table.

"It wasn't, just lonely. For a while, I'd talk to people

on the radio, the CB, but after a while, the tower must have come down. I couldn't find anybody, no matter how hard I tried. Maybe it froze and shattered, I don't know. After that, yeah, I think I went a little crazy."

"But you didn't leave it?"

"That's what's so funny. I couldn't leave! I tried so many times, crazy with the need to escape those same walls." She paused, stirred the pot she had the chicken cooking in, and scoffed to herself. "The hinges had frozen shut on the hatch. I couldn't get the damn door to open. I was stuck down there. I thought about suicide, but, well, I was raised Catholic. It's a sin."

And that was the end of her story, as far as she was concerned, Ann could see. "Thank you for telling me, Amelia."

"Thought you should know something about me." The woman with dark hair scraped back into the world's tightest bun and dark eyes was tough, often brusque, and her arms were covered in tattoos. But she worked hard and meant well. She didn't cause problems, and Ann could see now that she was shy more than anything. "Tell your parents dinner will be in 25 minutes. I have to put the dumplings in, let them cook for 15 minutes, and then I'll bring it all out to the dining room."

"Thanks, Amelia." Ann smiled at her as she left the kitchen and headed up the stairs. The house was filled with the scent of bay leaves and sage, some of her favorite smells. The plants grew in their backyard secret garden, and their freshness made their food amazing, even if it was only chicken or fish.

"Mom, Dad? Are you ready to eat?" she called softly and knocked.

"Come in, baby." Mary's voice was tinged with tears, and Ann could see her eyes and nose were red. She'd been crying. "Come here to me."

Ann did, and let her mother embrace her without complaint. "It's alright, Mom. Really. Maybe it's better this way."

"How? You're going to be married to some kind of barbarian!"

"Of course, he's not, Mom! He traveled across the galaxy, somehow. Have they explained that yet, Dad?"

"It's some kind of wormhole. Something about folding points in time and getting from point to point. Apparently, it only took them a couple of months to get here."

"Wow," Ann said, her thoughts on how far they must have come. "It's millions of light-years to the edge of our galaxy. They must have come from somewhere beyond there, for us not to know about them."

"I think Amanda would understand more about it than I do," he said, but then looked away. "Not that they'll ever explain it to her."

"You can, Dad, between the two of you, I'm sure you could figure it out."

"Not how to replicate it, I'm sure, but maybe how it works."

"I'm still here, you know," Mary snipped and Ann sat up with a laugh.

"Sorry, Mom. Look, I'm okay with this. I don't have a choice, and maybe I'll freak the fuck out tomorrow, but right now, I'm calm. I get why this has to happen, and I'm good with it."

"I wish I was as brave as you. You always were brave though. That's why you beat Rex at sports all the time."

"What?" Ann asked, her gaze on her Mom. "I don't know what you're talking about."

"Of course, you remember, honey. All those games you had during the school's field days, when you were little kids? You always beat him. He hated it, but Amanda and I used to laugh about it at the time. She thought it was good for him."

"I really don't remember that." She didn't like to play sports at all, how could she have been better than him?

"I'm surprised. But then, you'd always give him your ribbons and medals. He tried to take one once, after the principal gave it to you. He'd come to expect you'd give them to him. You socked him right in the eye and told him not to be rude." Mary laughed, and John joined her.

"I remember that," her father said. "I thought the

Wolfsons would sue us, but they thought it was funny too."

"Have you two been smoking weed or something?" Ann asked. She couldn't remember any of that, at all.

"No, honey, ask Amanda. She'll tell you it all happened," Mary said and got up from the bed, in a lighter mood now. "I was so upset when you didn't want to play sports, but you said it wasn't fair to Rex because you always beat him."

"Nope. Don't remember that either. I just remember I hated sports."

"Not when you were little. You wanted to play baseball with Rex, and track, and you loved volleyball. But then, you stopped playing, and I had to get used to it."

"It's just so weird that I can't remember," Ann said and tried her best. She remembered Elizabeth in a volleyball uniform but couldn't remember ever having played it at anything other than in her gym class.

"You were taking up for him, even then, Ann. It's not surprising."

"Hmm. Well, I can't take up for him anymore, it seems." She regretted it as soon as she said it.

"I'm so sorry, honey." Her mother's eyes filled with tears, and Ann knew she had to start all over again.

"Mom, stop." She wrapped her hand around her mom's face and looked at her. "It's alright. I'm going to make the most of this. I promise."

"I'm sure you will, honey. I don't like it either, but there's little choice, for any of us."

"I know, Dad. Mom, don't be upset. I'm not. I'm looking forward to the things that we can do to help our people. It's going to be alright, really."

She didn't know if that was true or not, but she wanted it to be. And she had no other choice. She could cry, and whine, and protest, but it would do no good. There was no higher authority to appeal to. He was the supreme commander, and he had chosen her.

She wondered, for a moment, if he'd been in other women's dreams. Or if it was some kind of connection that only they shared? She wasn't so romantic, or naïve enough, to think that he wanted her out of love. He didn't know her and there was only sex in her dreams. She didn't know if he had the same dreams, either. She might be the only one of them that had them.

There was no way of knowing anything, at this point, and there was nothing she could do about it. She wondered if Rex would be relieved. He wouldn't be stuck with her, after all. He'd said she was the best-looking woman their age around, but she'd wanted him to love her. He never seemed to really care about her though, now that she was being frankly honest with herself.

She wanted to be his wife, to have all of those teenage dreams come back to life, but for a moment, she let her delusions wash away. He'd be angry, more than likely, but only because he'd lost her. He wouldn't be angry about what would happen to her, or that she had no choice, he'd just be angry that he lost her.

Ann brushed a tear away and led her parents downstairs. Don't cry yet, she told herself, just wait, and maybe you can hold the tears off forever.

16

That night, she heard pebbles being thrown at her door again. Only this time, it was soon followed by a tap. Rex had climbed up the wall to get to her balcony. She smiled as she opened the doors and went out to meet him.

"You came, I didn't think you would." She hugged him, but he didn't seem as happy to see her.

"Yeah, I've come to think up an escape plan for you. We can't let you marry that scum." He sat down, his chin on his fist, lost in thought already.

"I… Rex, I can't escape. You'll all die. Don't you get that?" She sat down across from him at the white, wrought iron table and looked at him. "Your parents, mine, the people that work here, the ones that live in the district. We'll all die."

"Then we'll kick the bastards out," he cried, but not too loudly. He didn't want to get caught up here.

She drew the white cotton robe around her body and tried not to shiver. It wasn't cold, but Rex's refusal to see sense had chilled her. "Rex, honey. You can't. There's nothing we can do but enjoy whatever time we have left together."

"You mean…?" He looked hopefully for a moment, but when she shook her head, he frowned and slouched again. "Damn."

"I can't sleep with you, and then go off to a new man in a matter of days, Rex. I just can't." It was gross to her. She didn't care what other people did, but it wasn't for her.

"When will it happen?" he asked, his eyes now on the sky.

"I don't know. He didn't say."

"Some of the guys have said that his men are pissed. They want him to marry someone else, not you."

"What? They're all planning to take pure-blood women as their brides, aren't they? How is he any different for taking me?" She felt stupid, but it stung a little that his men didn't think she was an acceptable bride.

"I don't know, do I, Ann? I just know what they said. So, maybe this won't happen, maybe we can still be together."

Ann didn't hold out much hope of that. The man had seemed determined to have her. The threat he'd made proved that.

"I wish we could go back to the bunker," he said it softly, and Ann wasn't sure she heard him right.

"Seriously? After the way you hated it, you want to go back there?"

"It was all simple there, Ann. We weren't controlled, and life wasn't so bad. Not really, was it?"

"Well, you won the ignoring championship of the world down there, you barely acknowledged I existed, most of the time, but yeah. Life was simpler. And also boring. And not guaranteed. We had no promise of tomorrow down there."

"Like we do up here? The weather could change in an instant. The aliens could kill us all, anything could happen. We could get sick, anything."

"I know, but, still. It's not so bad up here, Rex. Even if I do have to marry an alien."

It sounded so odd to say it, and it reminded her of her earlier thoughts. "I thought you'd be mad."

"Oh, I am. They're stealing you from me, but unless I can come up with a plan, there's nothing to do about it." He kicked back, his arms over his chest, covered with his work clothes. He didn't have anything else.

That was something else she could work on when she married that alien, she thought. She could chip away at this notion that the wolves should be enslaved, with no free time or benefits to show for the work they did, other than the bare basics of life.

"Are you hungry? Do you want something to drink?" she offered and was disappointed when he grunted out that he didn't want anything. It came out petulant, like a spoiled child that was being appeased.

Maybe he was, but she didn't know what else to do. He reminded her of what her mother had said, about how she'd slugged him when he took a medal from her before she could offer it to him, as if it was his due.

"You know I wouldn't do it, if that threat wasn't over my head, right, Rex?" It was the only medal she could give him, right now. The truth.

"Sure. You'd totally give up being the queen of the planet to live with me in the shed. Others wouldn't believe you, but I do." His wink said the opposite.

"That's not fair, Rex, and you know it. I'm not, nor have I ever been, some fame-hungry, power-hungry tramp. I'm just doing what is right, that's all."

"Of course, you are, Ann. You always do." He brushed hair back from her face now and looked at her in the moonlight. "You're probably the only girl that ever did, our entire lives."

"Elizabeth and Maria were good too," she said softly, in love with the way his eyes shone in the darkness.

"Maybe. I didn't know them, but you, you were always good. You didn't even skip school."

"I didn't see the point. We'd be out soon enough, able to do what we wanted, and getting on with life."

"Sure, but it was nice to be out during the weekday. Like you were spying on this secret world that only adults and kids that had doctor's notes would ever see. It wasn't just the thrill of doing something I wasn't supposed to that I liked, it was seeing that side of the world. The side we never saw because we were always in school."

"That sounds, wow, I never thought of it like that." It sounded far more profound than maybe it really was, but she liked it, the way he described it.

"Even with a note, it didn't have that same secret quality to it. You were with your parents, accepted into the secret world, but if you weren't supposed to be there, if you were being delinquent, then it was like this whole new world." He smiled, a happy smile at his memories.

"I wish you'd have talked to me more back then."

"I couldn't. You were my nerdy neighbor, and I was too awesome for that."

"I think you mean you knew I wouldn't let you in my pants, just because of the sports you played." The words came out snarky, harsh, but his had stung too.

"Yeah, probably some of that too. Man, I remember,

Jennifer Harmon let me in her pants the day we met. She was brand new to school and hot as fuck."

"Seriously, Rex?" Ann sat up, disgusted.

"What? You're the one that's about to marry an alien, not me. Save the dramatics for someone that gets to marry you. I don't get that luxury."

"That's bullshit and you know it, Rex. You're just being petty again." She got up from the table and went to the door. "Look, there's not a lot we can do to change this, so don't go causing trouble. We just have to face reality. I wanted to be a part of your life for a long time. You had your chance, and you didn't take it in time. I hate it, I really do, but our time is past now. I have to think of the people that will get hurt if I refuse."

"Good to the end, aren't you, Ann?" He smirked, but he stood up and waltzed over to the railing. "I don't accept this, just so you know. I will change it. You will be mine."

She sighed as he disappeared, frustrated with him, as always. She knew a blood pressure monitor would explode if she wore one the entire time she was with him. Why did he always have to be such an ass?

She closed the doors quietly behind her and went to the bathroom to take the bath she'd been about to run when he interrupted her. She needed to relax, just for five minutes. She wanted to take that alien right out of her brain for just a little while and a nice hot bath would help her do that.

With a pleased breath, she sank beneath the water a few minutes later and tried to let her brain stop working. It didn't help. Every time she closed her eyes, she heard him say her name. Or felt his phantom touch from her dreams.

She wondered again if he had the same dreams she did. If they had done all of those things in that dream world, and he knew just how dirty she could be. She had no control in her dreams, no way of knowing that it was real. They just happened.

She needed him, wanted him, more than anything else on Earth, in those dreams, even when she was aware enough to know it was wrong. It didn't matter. She craved him when she was near. She remembered how her body had reacted when he'd come to the house earlier that day.

Every hair on her body, which wasn't many nowadays, stood on end. Then, other things had happened, things she'd ignored. Her nipples had gone tight as they prepared for his touch. And down there, in the place only she had ever touched once she was potty trained, that place had turned to liquid heat.

Her eyes had devoured him, longed for every inch of him to be naked in front of her, and ready to give her what she needed. But she'd controlled herself, she hadn't given anything away. That she knew of.

Even now, her body responded to the thought of him with eager desire, ready to be touched, and to touch. It was embarrassing, but she was alone, so that made it better. Not like earlier when it had happened in a room full of people.

What would it be like to be married to him? In her dreams, she was good, as long as he didn't touch her. She wanted him, yearned for him, to touch her, but if he didn't, she could cope. It was when he actually touched her that she lost her mind.

Not like when Rex touched her. His touched caused her heart to flutter in her chest, but little else. She didn't feel the burning desire, that low, hot, ache deep between her legs, that made her almost crazy with need. Rex didn't cause that at all.

Mainly, Rex caused her annoyance.

She could admit it now, now that she had no other choice in her life. Maybe her mom had been onto something earlier. Ann had given up sports so that Rex could excel and be the best in their school. She didn't remember it, but she had to believe what her mother told her. Maybe she'd been doing that for a long time, letting Rex win so that he could be happy.

She'd been infatuated with him most of her life, it would make sense that she would put her own needs after his. Even when he'd ignored her, she'd done things for him to try and cheer him up. She was always doing things for him, so he wouldn't have to, so he could stay in his room and mope. As he deserved to do.

He hadn't ever cared what she needed though, had he? He'd never even brought her a flower, she realized, and sat up now that the water had started to cool. As she scrubbed herself clean and washed her hair, she thought that maybe it wouldn't be so heartbreaking not to marry the boy after all.

Because that's what he was, really. A boy. Not a man. Real men didn't act like kids all the time and spout off about stupid revolution ideas. Damn, that was such a stupid notion of his. She wrapped her hair in a towel. She found a gift, wrapped up in a white box with red ribbon, sitting on her bed when she went back into her bedroom.

Wondering if Rex had read her thoughts, she sat down and opened the box to *see what* was inside. A portable, personal DVD player, with a memory stick full of movies and television shows! Oh my, now that was exciting! She hadn't seen any television or movies since the end came. None of them had had time to record or download anything, and it was oddly lacking in the entertainment department in the bunker. Her mom had a few old black and white films on her phone, they'd watched those a few times, but the phone's charger had stopped working after a few months.

"To my bride. May you sleep peacefully, tonight. I'll see you soon."

She frowned. It wasn't from Rex. Of course, it wasn't, she told herself. He wouldn't be that thoughtful, even if he had found it, he would have kept it for himself, as was his due.

She really shouldn't be such a bitch about him, she thought, but it was hard. For most of her life, she'd done whatever it took to make him happy, she'd put up with his moods, those awful moods that always looked so… romantic, in films. In real life, she'd often found herself wanting to kick him.

In the last couple of months, her eyes had really started to open about him. He wasn't some romantic figure, a poet in need of inspiration. He was just a jerk.

Ann wasn't sure if she was trying to convince herself or if this was just truth that she finally understood. She had no choice, she had to marry the alien, but she didn't have to hate Rex to do it, did she?

She put the memory card into the DVD player and started to go through the list of items she could watch. She couldn't stop thinking about Rex though. She felt as if she was on a constant roller coaster when it came to him. One minute she hated him, never wanted to speak to him again, and the next she wanted to have his babies while she promised to be his doormat forever.

She had a sneaky suspicion that, if the world hadn't ended and she'd been able to go off to the state university and get away from him, she'd have been over her infatuation with him a long time ago. Instead, she'd been thrown into close quarters with him for five years. Well, that was all over now, she said to herself, she had a new direction to go in, and Rex would have to be a part of the past. She was to be the alien's bride, and there wasn't a thing any of them could do about it.

17

*A*nn spent the next week in a haze, she didn't know when the alien would come for her, how long she had to prepare herself for it, mentally. She'd resigned herself to it the moment he announced his plans to marry her, but that didn't mean she wasn't worrying about it. Around the family and everyone else, she maintained a calm air, mainly to keep her mom from freaking out. But inside, she wanted to scream.

All of her life, she'd felt like a pawn, a piece in someone else's game, and now, she felt that even more. She had no control over her life, but she did have hopes that the man wouldn't be completely terrible to her. The dreams she had about him, oddly, reassured her. He wasn't always gentle in those dreams, but he wasn't cruel.

That helped to keep her terror at bay, anyway.

"What do you plan to do today, Ann?" her mother asked as they ate their breakfast by the pool. Some fruit, a couple of pancakes, and some juice were enough to fill her up.

"I don't know. It's hard to plan when I have no idea what this alien has in store for me."

"Well, you can't just hang around doing nothing. You'll drive yourself crazy that way." Mary smiled at her shocked daughter. "It does you no good if I'm distraught all the time, does it? Maybe we should go out into the city, have a look around at some of the places the aliens haven't raided yet."

"For what, Mom?" Ann was surprised at this new turn in her mother, and it made her uneasy. She had been the one in control, but now her mother had decided to stop panicking and just enjoy the time she had left with her daughter.

"I don't know, Ann. For whatever we can find I suppose. I hadn't really thought about what we could look for, I just thought it might be nice, like those times when you were little, and your dad would be with a client on the weekend."

"Ah, those trips into places just out of the city. You'd always buy me ice cream or candy." Ann smiled as memories flooded back. "I loved doing that. We'd always find the strangest places to go into."

"I loved all of those old places, the pharmacies that

had been there for generations that sold the oddest things. The antique shops."

"Those hats from the 40s!" Ann's smile grew bigger as she remembered picking up soft velvet and lace hats that hadn't been worn in generations. "I loved those hats."

"They were lovely. It's such a shame we don't wear those things anymore. Women used to be so... decorative." Mary realized what she'd said and looked at Ann with an embarrassed laugh. "Well, I guess they were decorations, weren't they?"

"Do you think that's what this alien wants with me? Decoration?" It was a worry that she couldn't shake. She wanted to participate in the rebuilding of the world, have a place in it. Not necessarily to be known throughout history for it, but she did want a place in the next chapter of Earth's saga.

"I don't know. I think they want babies, most definitely. Your father says their DNA is almost exactly the same as ours. So, it's not like you'd be breeding with something with tentacles or anything." Mary shuddered and stood up. "Let's get dressed and head out, shall we?"

"Sure, I'll meet you downstairs in ten minutes." Ann ran up to her room, put on a pair of jeans, a long black blouse that came down to her hips, and a pair of hiking boots. If she was going to be climbing around old shops, good shoes would be needed.

She tied her hair up in a ponytail and met her mom downstairs a few moments later. "Ready?"

"Yes. Let's go. Your father's already left. He has a meeting with the aliens today and they sent a transporter." They went out to their own transporter and Ann put her hand on the panel that would unlock the vehicle after her palm was scanned. It would work for her parents, or her, nobody else, which was better than any key and lock mechanism, she thought as she climbed in.

She drove in silence, her hand on the lever, as she looked for a place that hadn't been picked over by the aliens and their crew of wolf servants, or by other humans. She'd been to most of the shops by the courthouse, so she headed out, to the outskirts of the city.

"Oh, these look good," Mary said as Ann stopped the vehicle and they got out.

"Just think, Mom, it's all ours for the taking. We can have whatever we want now, nobody will ask a dime for it."

"Isn't it odd?" Mary said as they walked in through an empty door, the place covered in dust, fallen timbers, and the smell of mildew. Still, it was a lingerie store and the women went inside. "We used to put so much value on everything. We could have it all, for a price."

"Now, we can take whatever we want." Ann spotted some bras wrapped in plastic and went to look them over. She found some in her size and took those, not that she needed them right now, but she might in the future. That's what she told herself, but she knew she really just liked the look of black lace and sapphire blue ribbons on the things.

"You might want to look for things that you'll need if you get pregnant, Ann." Her mom told her, and Ann saw Mary was standing in front of a display for maternity underwear.

"Oh." She looked at the panties, and nursing bras, bemused. "Do you think?"

"Yes. Just in case. We don't know what will happen, do we?" But neither of them moved to pick up the garments. Doing that would have made it all too real, and both of them turned away.

Ann didn't want to think about pregnancy in a time when there were no doctors, no medicine, and nobody to help if she needed it. The aliens might have the technology needed to make it all safe, but she didn't know if they did. They had all kinds of great stuff, she knew that, but were there doctors?

"Let's just, no, let's not worry about that right now." Ann walked away and went to find a bag to put her new bras in.

Suddenly, it was all more than she could handle, and she sobbed softly. Her mother was there in an instant, her arms around her daughter to block the world out.

"I'm so sorry, baby. Maybe we should have stayed in the bunker."

"No, Mom, it was what we needed to do. And this is what I need to do." Ann pulled away, wiped at her face, and sniffed the tears away. "I just lost control for a second. I can do this, don't worry."

"Baby, you're my little girl. No matter how big you get, or how old, you're always my little girl. I'd give my life for you. You know that. If you don't want to do this, say the word. Your father and I will take you away and we won't look back."

"But, Mom, that's my job, to take care of you two! I can't let you die because of me, or any of the others either. No, I have to do this."

"It's a vicious circle isn't it?" Mary picked up a pair of panties from a stack on the counter and wiped at Ann's face. "You want to protect us, we want to protect you, and none of us win except the aliens."

"Our overlords." It sounded ridiculous to say it out loud, but it was the truth. "If you get to live, and the Wolfsons, and everyone else, well, it's worth it, Mom. I just had a moment."

"Totally understandable, Ann," Mary assured her and let the panties fall to the floor. The silky green panties fluttered to the ground, forgotten as they left the store. "I saw an antique shop just down the street. Let's see if they have any hats."

Ann laughed and left the store with her mother.

* * *

WHEN THEY ARRIVED HOME, they found a group of men in the driveway, all dressed in the soldiers' uniforms the aliens all wore. That's all Ann had ever seen them in, anyway, other than the supreme leader. Ann and her mother quietly hurried out of the transporter and walked into the house.

There they found the place as quiet as a church on Monday. There were no servants in sight, and neither one felt it appropriate to call out for John. They looked at each other and then walked down to the living room, with an arm around the other's waist. John was there and so was the alien, Rager. That's what his name was.

"Good afternoon, ladies! Out for a bit of shopping, were you?" Rager stood up, and Ann finally placed his accent. It sounded British for some reason. Why would an alien have a British accent? "Come and join us, won't you?"

Ann saw two cups of hot tea, one with some kind of cream in it, on the table in front of one of the couches. "Hello, how are you?"

"I'm great, Ann. Thank you. How are you?" His eyes were hungry for her, and ate her up, despite the fact that her parents were in the room.

"I'm good, thank you." She refused to call him Rager, it sounded ridiculous.

Where fear had been her constant companion lately, anger now took over. Who was he to come in here like everything was normal, and he hadn't just blackmailed her into marriage? He acted as if they'd had a long courtship and now were on the cusp of uniting as one after a long wait. Damn, if it didn't make her angry!

She had to be polite though, she didn't want to rile the man. His sheer size quelled most of her anger down to a simmering rage. He could just swallow her, and there'd be nothing left, she thought as she took a seat beside her mother on the opposite couch.

"Good. You can get ready now. Today's the day." His smile was broad and showed off straight, white teeth.

Her body responded to that smile, and she leaned forward, despite her efforts to remain aloof. "The day for what?"

She blinked at him, hoping he didn't mean that day. The one she'd tried not to think about.

"The day we become mates, Ann. If you want to get that lovely dress of yours, I want to show you the house I've had prepared for us, and then we can get on with the ceremony."

Ann just blinked again. "Okay."

She couldn't move, she couldn't think, all she could do was stare at him. She sat there like a lump until her mother stood up and took her hand. "Come on, baby. Let's do this."

She wanted to scream profanities, to tell her mom to back off, to tell her father to put a stop to this, but she didn't. She just followed behind her mother and went up to pick up the bag she'd thrown the dress in once he'd left all those days ago.

"Mom, I don't want to do this. I know I have to, but I don't want to."

"I know, honey. Do you want to run? We can go, just you and me…" It was the tears in her mother's eyes that slapped Ann in the face and brought her back to reality.

"No. I have to do this."

She picked the bag up and squared her shoulders. "I can do this. I can."

THIRTY MINUTES later she was outside of a house that looked as if it belonged on a plantation in the Mississippi delta. It was a sprawling mansion, with columns, white marble, and a circular driveway of white gravel that must have been a nightmare to keep up. She realized it was the kind of home she'd dreamed of having when she was a little girl and didn't understand the history of such places.

"Isn't it gorgeous?" he asked as he stopped the transporter he was driving, and the glass came up.

"Yes," Ann said, her brain still rather empty.

"Let me show you inside." He helped her get out of the transporter and she followed along behind him. Thick oak double doors opened, and she walked into a house filled with antiques and alien technology.

She saw things that gave off the signature blue light of the alien technology, and old things that gave off no light at all. She couldn't take in what it all was but saw one that must be some kind of screen in a room to her right. Figures moved on the screen, but she couldn't hear anything. Small round robotic vacuums moved around the floors, but not all of them swept the floor. Some mopped, others carried things, heading in directions she didn't know.

"I'll show you the bedroom later. For now, I want you to see the garden I've had created for you." He led her through many rooms, and then out of a door.

They were standing on some kind of patio, and spread out for acres beyond were gardens, flower gardens, vegetable gardens, a greenhouse, and a potting shed. There were plants of almost every variety, in pots, in the ground, everywhere. Beyond that, rolling green hills were speckled with animals.

"Are those horses? And cows?" Ann gasped and walked to the edge of the patio.

"Yes, our engineers finally raised some with their ancestors' DNA. We found some frozen before we thawed the planet out and extracted their DNA to create these beautiful creatures."

"So, you've been here for a while then?" Ann asked, but she wasn't sure she meant to. She was too focused on the pretty blond horse and the white cow speckled with spots that almost looked blue.

"Yes, a year or so," he revealed as he came to stand beside her. "Do these things make you happy?"

"They do. Yes." She lost interest in the animals and the garden the instant he came to stand beside her. Awareness, longing flooded into her blood and she looked up at him.

"I've had you so many times in our dreams, Ann. It's going to be so nice to finally have you for real."

"Pardon?" She blinked some more, stunned at what he'd said. That didn't stop her from leaning into him when his hands went around her back and pulled her close.

She wanted to fight him, to tell him to take his hands off of her. But she couldn't. Not when she wanted only to crawl closer to him.

"It's what your people call ESP, I suppose. When we find our mates, we can share our dreams and thoughts with them. And I want every one of those dreams we've had to come true." His head came down, and his lips traced up her neck.

A shudder went through Ann's body and her hands went up around *his neck*. Not to push him away. Oh no, she wanted more. All of it. All of him.

18

"I can't believe this is happening," Mary whispered as she looked at Ann.

Ann heard the way her mother's voice wobbled and tried not to look at her. If she did, she'd cry. Not tears of joy either. She was terrified, now that the moment was at hand. She would be brave, she would get through this, if only her mother didn't cry.

"Hush now, Mary," her father said gently and took his wife in his arms. "We all have to be strong now."

"Thank you, Dad," Ann whispered and tried not to let them see her wipe a tear away.

The ceremony was to take place in the garden, in a lovely little hidden spot, full of roses and columbine flowers. There wouldn't be many people, so the 6-foot space would hold them all. He'd shown it to her before he sent her up to change. Her parents had arrived, and by that point, Ann had her dress on. She'd been ready then, in charge of herself, even if his words did ring in her ears.

All of those dreams, they'd shared them? It was the next best thing to real? Her cheeks and chest burned with heat as she thought about it all over again. At least that distracted her from her mother's tears. She could get past that moment, even if it was something stupid like shame that did it.

"Okay, let's get this over with." She stood up in the dress she'd planned to marry Rex in and looked at her parents with wide eyes. She could face this, because it meant they would live. They would have another day to fight for the life they'd hung on to these last few years. They would continue to be survivors, as long as she knuckled down and got through this.

Her mom pulled the short train of her dress up so she wouldn't fall down the marble stairs, and her dad kept his arm at her elbow. The shoes were a little taller than she thought they were, and she wobbled on her way down. At least, that's the excuse she made.

Her mom wore the dress, and her dad the suit, the clothes she'd found for them, but neither of them really looked happy about this. It was not a joyous moment. It was a forced moment, a submission to a stronger power. Fuck, it sounded so abysmal, she thought, as she headed out to the garden.

At least she was attracted to him. She couldn't deny that, no matter how much she wanted to. She wanted him, wanted to know if he was as good in reality as he was in her dreams. He was not only foreign; he was from another planet. For all she knew, the man was a sex god. Or maybe he was terrible at it. Either way, she'd do her best to get through it.

Not that she had any doubt that she'd want it. Maybe he'd cast a spell on her, or he was controlling her with ESP stuff, she wasn't sure, but as she came near to him, her brain calmed. Then her body went on full alert because, holy cow, he was so hot.

She turned into a 15 year old girl again, with all the innocent want that came with that age. She wanted him, like she'd never wanted anyone else, and it made her feel goofy all over again. She smiled at him as she came to stand beside him. There was another tall man behind him, a man almost as hot as he was, but she only had eyes for him.

Suddenly, she wasn't afraid anymore, she wasn't angry, she was just ready to take him to bed.

Another man, smaller than the other two men, but still taller than anyone in her family, was towards the back of the small alcove. The shape was created with hedges, and rose vines grew in the midst of it all. It was a pleasant little spot, and a nice place to have the ceremony.

The man spoke in some language she didn't understand, and Ann shifted on her feet. Rager made a sound and the man shifted into English.

"Sorry, sir." He cleared his throat, and looked at Ann. "My name is Agnar, I will join you as a mate to Rager. Do you agree to this?"

Ann looked down to where their hands were joined. She hadn't realized that he'd taken her hands in his until then. She saw the tattoos on the insides of her wrists and looked over at his arms. She could see tattoos there, but couldn't make out what they were.

"Ann?" Agnar asked her again, and she looked up at him.

"Yes?" She gazed at him in confusion, the question completely forgotten as she looked at their hands.

"Do you agree to be made Rager's mate?"

"What? Oh, yes, I do." She looked up to see amused eyes in a face that should make her tremble in fear. His hair was pulled back and his face was open for her to see.

"Good. Rager, do you agree to be made Ann's mate?" the man asked, and Ann watched Rager's eyes flick to him before he answered.

"Yes, I do."

"Good. Open your hands."

Rager opened his hands, and Ann followed his lead. She felt a weird sadness when he took his hands away, but his presence itself was a drug, and that was enough for now. Agnar turned away and took something from a table behind him.

"Rager, this is your modalla, your energy that will bond you to Ann." The man put something that looked like an orange marble that glowed with a white-hot light into Ann's hands. She expected the thing to burn, but it didn't. She looked at it, intrigued by the marble that looked so small but felt so heavy in her hand.

"Ann, this is your modalla, your energy that will bond you with Rager." He placed a dark brown marble in Rager's hand, one that glowed as hotly as the one in her hand. "Close your hands, and kiss now please."

Ann leaned forward and closed her hands around the marble, just as their lips met. Her eyes flew open as something invaded her mind, her heart, every single part of her body and soul. She felt something entwine around her, until it felt like her breath had been stolen away. And then she could see him, with the same expression she felt on her face.

She knew him, felt him, inside of her. At the same time, she felt as if she was inside of him. Did this mean they were one? Was this why they called it mates? They were now mates, for eternity?

"It is done. I wish you joy in your new life, and a lot of productivity. May you find the way."

Ann leaned back, shocked at what had just happened.

She could still feel him, lingering in the back of her mind. What had just happened? She wasn't sure she wanted to know. She turned her head, saw her mother and father, and smiled at them. It's okay, her smile told them, and they both relaxed.

"Please, John, Mary, if you would join us for dinner. It's traditional to eat a meal with the parents on this day. Mine are far away, too far to come, so if you would do me the honor, I would greatly appreciate it."

"Of course, Rager. Thank you." Her father smiled up at the giant she had just been mated to and led his wife away.

"Thank you, Ann. I know this must be difficult. I didn't realize you didn't know the dreams were, shall we call them, real? I thought you'd agreed to this; I am a buffoon."

She gaped at him as they walked back into the house and into a very large dining room. "No, I didn't know. Thank you."

Had he only just learned that? Had he figured it out during the ritual that mated them? She scurried around in her memories and found a few that weren't hers. The scent of a woman that she realized was how she smelled to him, the moment he'd seen her, that first day they'd been captured. He'd been the soldier that told them they were free to go. He'd seen her with her father, in the transporter as well, and it seemed those were memories he treasured.

It was disconcerting, to know she shared someone's memories, and that they would know things about each other now. She wasn't sure she liked it, but she did know one thing, for certain. Rager was now hers for the rest of her life, and there wasn't a woman on Earth, or elsewhere, that would break that. The same as she wouldn't leave him for another man. Not even Rex.

The dinner took two hours, and it was a real feast. Turkey, ham, it was all available, as were delicious vegetable dishes that she couldn't identify because her mind was taken up with nothing but him. Her parents left soon after, and he took her up to the bedroom.

"So soon?" she asked but didn't protest.

"Do you want to wait? We can, if you prefer, but I must warn you, I'm not sure I can wait very long."

"No, I don't want to wait. I want… well, I want you." She knew no other way than to be straightforward with him about it. She was his mate now, and she couldn't deny that, even if she wanted to.

"You are so fragile, not like the women from my world." His finger slid the right sleeve of her dress away. "So delicate and seductive."

"I'm only me," she said but couldn't breathe. He was in her head, deep in her mind, and all she wanted was to be his.

She knew it didn't make any sense, other than they were connected somehow, and apparently had been since they'd first met. The modalla had joined them, in some alien way, but they'd dreamed together for months now. She barely knew him, but she knew what made him groan her name. Ann's knees went weak and she sank down to the bed.

He sank down in front of her and slid her dress up her legs slowly. She watched him, her breath held until the moment his fingers touched the soft skin of her thighs. Air forced out of her lungs as his skin came into contact with hers, and she heard him make a sound of his own.

"You have beautiful thighs, my dear."

She looked down to see his gaze was on her skin, and he wasn't joking. His fingers teased up a little to brush beneath her dress, at the very top of her thighs, before he slid them back down again. She fought to breathe again, desire a drum in her veins, in her ears, as he leaned forward to kiss each thigh in turn. His lips were hot, a slight pressure against the spot where her thighs met just above the stocking.

"I'd like to see them naked, however. Do you mind?" His gaze met hers and she shook her head, she wanted this now. She could hate herself later, but for now, she didn't want anything else but his lips, wherever he wanted to put them. "Good."

His fingers looped around elastic lace and removed the stocking she'd put on only a short while before. The garments quickly disappeared behind him, and Rager settled in, his body now a wedge that kept her legs open. "I want to make you happy, Ann. I'm not an overly cruel man, so please, don't be afraid of me."

"I'm, I'm not," she gasped, her legs relaxing as he put each one over his shoulders. She knew what he wanted to do, he'd done it so many times in her dreams, and she eased back, her palms out flat behind her to steady her. Would it feel the same in real life?

"Good. Now, let me please you."

Ann's eyes closed and she sank into some kind of oblivion as his lips parted her folds to explore her hidden secrets. It was better than her dream, far more vivid, far more personal when his tongue slid into her, and then up, to that precious spot he'd only ever touched in her dreams.

"Fuck," she spit the word out, the one she so rarely used, but she couldn't help herself. Her fingers dug into his hair and her hips began to dance as he found a rhythm, the only rhythm that would take her where he wanted to send her.

His hair was silky, long enough to tug on, and she did just that as he gave her all the attention she could have ever craved. "Rager…"

"Hmmm?" she heard him say, and gasped again.

It felt so good when he did that there, so very good.

"Nothing. Just don't stop. Please don't stop."

"Mmhmm." He did it again, and she couldn't help it. Something turned inside out inside of her, and the world exploded.

Her fingers tightened in his hair, and she heard another satisfied hum from down below, but she didn't care. She was too busy chasing a sensation she'd never felt before. Total bliss. It was so worth waiting for.

Rager drove her on, higher, again, with each lash of his tongue against her center, with each new hum, and all she could do was hang on and hope she couldn't die from it. When he finally let her down, she was certain the world would be black, colorless, because she'd sucked it all up when the world exploded inside of her.

"You lie there and pant, my dear, I'm going to get undressed." Rager chuckled softly and stood up.

Ann was too tired to open her eyes, but when he came back, totally nude, she sat straight up. "That can't go in me! It's as big as my arm!"

"Oh, it can, my dear, and quite snugly too. We'll just have to go slow to start with. Sit still, let me get this dress off of you. I want to look at what you've had hidden from me all this time."

She did as instructed and leaned forward when he pulled the dress away. He'd seen her naked for months in her dreams, so she didn't bother to hide herself from him.

"As beautiful as I knew you would be, my lovely." His fingers traced down her face, and when he reached her neck, he lingered, his eyes narrowed to watch her response.

He gently pushed her back to the bed covered in a luxurious red duvet and followed her down. He didn't climb over her, he just leaned over. His fingers traced down her collar bone, to the peak at the tip of her breast. Dusky rose and tight, the bud grew tighter as his finger circled it.

"Oh, I do like that," she whispered before she closed her eyes to revel in the sensation. A slight movement, more weight pressed into the bed, and then his wet mouth was over her left nipple. "Fuck!"

It came out again, but Ann couldn't stop the word. The wet heat of his mouth on her was too good, and she wanted more. He teased at her, then shifted to the other, before he moved back again.

Every part of her was filled with need, the only thing that mattered was more pleasure, and she knew that. She wanted it. She wanted him.

"Please, make it stop."

He let her nipple pop out of his mouth on a wet kiss and looked up at her. "Make what stop?"

"This ache! I want to die, I want to live, it's everything, fuck, I can't stand it. Please?" She held her hand out to him, and she watched as he came up to the bed.

"Are you sure? I wanted to take so much more time with you."

"I might die if you make me wait anymore, please. Just make me feel good."

"I only want to please." He spoke softly as he slid his hands under her hips to position her body for him. He held her with one hand then and used the other to guide himself to her entrance.

Ann held her breath, unsure of what this would feel like. It wasn't unpleasant, she thought as he slid into her, only a little at first. She shifted when she felt him spread her open, and her eyes went wide. It felt like being invaded, but she wanted this invasion, his invasion, of her.

Another moment, another slide in, and then he stopped. There was a tight spot inside of her, some barrier that she could feel him against. She felt a slight sting when he pressed a little harder against it and wondered if it would be bad. She'd heard it hurt, that it felt like you were being torn in two, but she didn't know.

"Breathe, Ann, you have to breathe if I'm going to make it inside you."

She looked at him, afraid of the pain that might come.

"It might hurt this first time, it might not. After that, it won't hurt again, not unless I'm careless, that is. And I don't ever plan to do that to you. So, just breathe, and let me inside you."

She shook her head in agreement and forced herself to take a breath. She moved when she felt her body relax and put her hands on his shoulders. Her hands gripped the hard muscles covered in silky skin. He was beautiful, every part of him a man, a human man, but a man that had been sculpted to perfection.

She didn't have anymore time to think about it, because he pressed deeper, harder, and the barrier broke that kept them apart. She cried out as pain ripped through her, but it didn't last very long. He had frozen when she made the first sound, but he'd made it past the point that mattered.

"Go on, more, please." She pulled her nails out of his skin; he hadn't even uttered a protest at that, she thought. He knew she was in pain and absorbed the moment for her, without protest.

When she began to take tentative stabs at moving, he soothed her with a kiss in the palm of her hand. The man was huge after all, even propped on his elbows he had to be careful. She tried to wrap her legs around his waist, and though he wasn't overweight, she could barely cross her ankles. The man was just that big.

She studied him, the broad expanse of his chest, the

way his muscles bunched when he moved, and ran her fingers down his smooth cheek. She looked up into his eyes and saw… happiness.

Ann wasn't sure why she didn't expect it, but she didn't. She smiled back at him, and that's when he began to move again.

"You're with me again. We can get back to enjoying each other now."

Every inch of him was familiar, yet she still couldn't believe it. She knew the dreams had been vivid, but this detailed? She even knew where the freckle was on his right shoulder and smiled when she saw it.

He shifted again, took more weight on his elbows, adjusted his hips, and began to slide into her. Deeper, so much deeper. She hadn't realized she could open that much, but she took every inch of his giant length. When she was impaled on him, had every inch of him inside her, she closed her eyes, and relaxed into the bed.

She dug her feet into the bed and began to move with him, in time with him. Over and over their hips met only to separate slightly as he pulled away. Each pull out and every push in stroked some new place in her, until he found that place deep inside, the one that got her attention.

"There, oh fuck, right there. More…" but she couldn't speak again. She was too caught up in the sensation as Rager drove into her, again and again.

She could smell the scent of his skin as it heated up, the smell that was only him, and tasted it on her lips when she reached up to kiss his chest. She wanted to know what he tasted like and it was all she could reach of him.

She felt him grinding into her, his cock inside of her, his pubic bone against her clit, over and over, until she couldn't take anymore. Her nipples scraped against his chest, and that was the spark that set her off. She exploded around him, tight and then tighter, as she forgot her own name.

"I can't hold back," he groaned as she spasmed around him, and he shot into her with a spasm of his own.

She rode the waves, and the waves that came after as he lost himself inside her. Gasping, sweating, they exploded together all over again, too caught up in each other to make it stop.

week later, and Ann had learned the ins and outs of her new home. She wandered around freely as nothing was locked. There was no part of the house hidden from her. She was the supreme leader's mate, his wife, and was allowed to wander as she chose.

She loved the new house, even if it was too palatial, and had fallen in love with both the horse and the cow in the pasture. Rager told her that he planned to have a real farm here, that everyone would eventually be required to produce food of some kind, as the districts spread out. She liked that idea and thought it was a good idea.

She saw her parents when she chose to and saw her mother a couple of days after the night that they were made mates. Her mother's relief when she walked into their house almost brought tears to Ann's eyes, but she held herself in check. She couldn't describe why she smiled like she did, but her mother could guess.

All she'd said was that she was glad it was working out well, and Ann agreed. She'd seen Amanda and talked with her. Amanda had been worried too, she'd said, but now, she could see a happiness in Ann that she'd never thought she'd see. She'd used the word contentment, and Ann had to agree.

She was contented. Happy with what life had brought her. She wanted to hate herself, to hate her new mate, but she couldn't. Maybe one day, but right now? She just wanted to spend every moment with him that she could.

Because Rager spent most of his day at work, either with the district leaders, or with his men, she usually only saw him at night. He'd go in to work before the sun came up and come home well after it had set. It was a little lonely for her, but she'd made friends with the cook, Angela, and with the head housekeeper, Alice.

They were sisters and had survived the cataclysm in a cave somewhere. There'd been little food, but Angela had managed to find some cold-weather gear before the real snow started, and she'd been able to go out and forage for them. Ann wrote their stories down, the same as she did all the stories she'd learned so far, and added it to her file.

Their nights were spent having meals, swimming in

the small pool to one side of the garden, and in bed. That was her favorite part, but it wasn't just the sex. He'd talk about his plans for the future, and how they wanted to bring the Earth back to life.

He'd told her the maps of the world had changed, that there was a new mountain range in the middle of the country, and that most of the east coast had disappeared beneath the water once the ice thawed out enough to bring the planet back to normal. There were countries that no longer existed, not because they were empty, but because they, too, had disappeared beneath the water.

It was all very sad, but the plan that Rager had, to create small districts that would spread out over time, was a really good one. Families would be formed, and in time, people would be allowed to move out to wherever they chose, so long as they could be self-sufficient.

She didn't ask him about the future for the wolves, and he didn't mention them. That would be for another time, she'd decided, when they trusted each other more. She wasn't afraid he'd be angry or distrust her, but she didn't want to rock the boat. Life was peaceful, far more peaceful than she'd thought it would have turned out, and she wanted to hold onto that for a while longer.

He also explained his accent, and the accent of the other soldiers. Some had American accents, some had French, English, German, and many other accents.

"We were all taught one language, on our way here. I was assigned English, so I was taught to speak it with an English accent. Later, those that hadn't learned English were taught the American version. And we loved to watch the American movies and television programs that we picked up as we traveled here. So, I was originally given English, while others were given a different language. That's why we all sound different."

"I see," she'd said. It did make sense, but it still made her smile.

"What's that smile about?" he'd asked and she'd laughed.

"Nothing, I'm just trying to picture a bunch of aliens watching television programs in space."

"It's not that hard, surely?" But he'd tickled her, and the conversation had soon turned to passion. As all of their conversations did.

Now, she was in her garden, happily waiting for him to come home. She had come out earlier to explore her plants and to put a few seedlings into pots. Rager brought them home from one of his trips to the ship and had asked her to take care of them. They were baby tomatoes, she decided, as she put the plants into pots. They'd have to go in the garden when they got a little bigger.

She'd been working quietly for an hour, when she heard voices outside. She knew it couldn't be Rager, so she kept putting seeds into pots. It was probably only the servants, or some of the soldiers that patrolled the grounds.

"But, why did he have to be mated to her?" one male voice said, tinged with a Russian accent. "Her DNA is muddied, mixed with Neanderthals. The other woman, her blood is pure alien from the last time our people came here."

Ann froze. This wasn't their first time here? And who was this other woman the speaker wanted Rager to marry instead of her? She should have told the men she was there, but curiosity got the better of her, and she stayed still.

"Because he liked her, stupid. He saw her the day she arrived, and that was it."

"He should have thought about the future. What will his children be like with her? The other woman would have given us superior children."

"She didn't want to leave Holland; he didn't want to be mated to her. Why's that so hard to understand?"

"We're being assigned mates," the other soldier muttered, and Ann knew this was the real problem. He hadn't been given a choice, but his leader had. That was the way of things now, however.

"Be glad you aren't at home, doofus. I heard the fires are raging even worse now, that they're unstoppable."

"That might be preferable. Have you seen the woman

they've assigned me? I think she's in her 50s, not her 40s like she claimed. Fuck. He got such a beauty, and I get an old hag."

"Just be glad you were given someone and stop moaning about it all. I need to check on her cow, someone might try to steal that thing if she keeps leaving it in the pasture like that."

"Yes, boys. Please go tend to my mate's cow. Oh, and Girlian? Don't you worry about who my wife is. I suggest you shut the fuck up from now on and do your fucking job instead. Or I'll send you back up to the ship and have you sent home. Understand?"

"Yes, sir. Sorry, sir. Have a good day, sir." Ann could hear their boots as they marched away. She smiled, even if they had irritated her. Rager was home, that made everything okay. Even if she knew she should hate him, it didn't mean she could.

"I'm in here," she called out to him and stood up when he ducked into the shed.

"I thought you might be in here. Heard that, did you?"

"Oh, yes. Poor you, mated to me when you could have some Dutch princess by your side."

"I have you, that's all the princess I could ever want, my dear." He leaned down and kissed her, even though she had dirt everywhere, even in her hair. She laughed and pulled away to wipe a speck of dirt from his nose.

"I'm glad you think so." She leaned into his embrace and wondered what had happened to the girl that had been so in love with Rex. It seemed she was gone, and Ann wondered if she would ever come back. She looked up into his orange tiger eyes, and then looked away. Rex would just have to stay a secret. Somehow. She didn't see her new husband letting her go any time soon.

"Are you going to your mother's today?" Rager asked as he dressed the next morning.

Ann watched him from their bed, her eyes still sleepy, but she liked to be up with him in the mornings. "Yes, I'm taking her some of those tomato plants. We have far too many."

"Good. I have some other stuff for them, I'll have one of the fellows put it in your transporter."

"Alright. Thank you."

He came to her, leaned down over her, and smiled. "For what?"

"For thinking of them. I know you don't have to."

"Ah, but they gave me you. I'll have to continue to thank them, don't you think?"

"Maybe so. They deserve it though. Everyone does, I guess."

"Perhaps. I'll see you tonight. I won't be late." He pecked a soft kiss on her lips that turned into something more, as it did every time he touched her, but he pulled away. "I may get back sooner. We'll have to see."

"You could just tell them to wait, you know?" She wrapped her arms around his neck and tried to pull him back.

With a laugh, he broke away and pulled his cuffs down over the circular tattoos on his arm. She'd studied the intricate circles more than once, but they still meant nothing to her.

"I'll see you tonight," she called out as he opened the door. For a moment, he turned, winked at her, then walked out into the dark of the hallway.

Ann went back to sleep for an hour, and then got up. She planned the dinner for that night with Angela, and then made sure her transporter was packed. By the time she made it to her parents' home, her father was gone for the day, and Mary was home alone. But she had an army of servants to keep her company and didn't mind that.

"I'm so happy to see you," Mary said when Ann came in, her arms loaded with plants. "It's just not the same without you here."

"You say that every time I come, Mom." She pecked her mom's cheek and walked back to the backdoor.

"Have someone plant these, Mom. They're tomato plants."

"Oh, that will be good! Put those down and let me see you." Mary spun Ann around, looked at the white dress with gold sandals that she had on with appreciation, and smiled. "He's still treating you well then."

"Oh, yes. Oh, and electricity is guaranteed now. Some of the wolves got the power plants back up and running."

"Thank goodness. Those solar panels are great, but we have to be so careful about what we use."

"I know. I'm glad about that too."

"At least we aren't in some of those places that don't even have solar panels."

"You're right, Mom. What are you having for lunch?"

"Chicken quesadillas. Just something simple to tide me over."

They were walking back into the house and Ann moved to let her mother go first. Something happened and her mother fell and knocked her head against the doorframe before she slumped into Ann's arms.

"Mom! What happened?" Ann let her mother down to the floor and looked her over. She had a cut over her eye and Ann called out for Amelia.

"I'm fine, honey, it was just a dizzy spell. Let me up. I'll go upstairs and clean this up."

"Mom, seriously, what's wrong?" Ann sat back as her mother pushed away from her.

"It's nothing, Ann, really. Now, go to the kitchen. I'll be down in a few minutes."

Mary shooed Ann away, and Ann went but she did it reluctantly. Amanda was in there with Rex. She hadn't seen him since that night in her room and now he was there, with a sneer on his face.

"Oh, and here comes the alien fucker, home to lord it over us all," Rex said with so much venom Ann almost felt as if he'd physically attacked her.

"Rex!" Amanda slapped her son and stood up. "You take that back!"

"No, Mom. It's true. She's fucking an alien so she can be the queen of the world." He stood up, did a dramatic twirl and tucked his folded hands under his chin to blink at her. "And you've graciously graced us with… your grace. So sweet."

"You think it's so great being his mate, Rex? His people hate me, they think I'm beneath them, and then there's you, sneering at me for something I had no choice in." It came back to her that Rager said he hadn't known she didn't want to be mated to him. Then why the ultimatum? To get over any objections her father might have? That made sense, but right now, all she wanted to do was slap Rex's snarky face.

"They think you're beneath them?" he asked, incredulous. "You're pure-blood."

"Apparently, there's more pure than even my blood. They were here before…" she paused when he leaned closer. What had she just revealed? Was it a secret?

"Thanks for that information, Ann. My organization can use it. But you're still disgusting, and I hope you die in childbirth!" He stormed away then, and Ann couldn't say anything to him.

"Ann, oh my darling girl, I'm so sorry for what Rex just said. I'm so sorry." Amanda rushed to her side and led her to the table where they all used to work to prepare family meals together. What had happened, what had she done so wrong? She'd only protected her people.

Her eyes filled with tears, and she let them spill. She wanted to go back to those simpler days, when Rex's tantrums weren't so bad, when she believed there could be a decent future for them all. Now, Rex wanted her to die and hated her.

"He's not taking this well at all," she said, finally.

"No. He's not. I'm worried about him, to be honest. Since you were married, mated, to the alien, he's gotten worse. I don't know what to do."

"I don't either," Ann said and dropped her head to her arms to sob. She cried tears she hadn't known she had as she sat there with Amanda.

Amanda tried to make her smile, tried to ease her tears, and then finally just wrapped her arm around Ann. "I'm so sorry, honey. I wish I could make this all go away or be better somehow."

"Thank you, Amanda. I know there isn't a lot you can do. And you did so much. You were like a second mom to me for so long. I know you want to help, but I think you need to focus on Rex. He's going to get himself into trouble if he keeps on."

"I worry about that boy."

Ann stood up, grabbed a towel and dried her face. She straightened her back bone, and sniffed one last time. "I can't do anything to help him. I don't know what would help him. I would if I could, but he seems determined to stay on this course of hatred. It makes no sense, Amanda. I know he hates being a servant, but this hatred? It's insane."

"I know, honey. I guess we'll just have to hope he doesn't take it further."

Her mother came back in, saw Ann's red face, and assumed it was because of her fall. "Ann! Baby, I'm fine! Don't be so upset!"

She rushed to Ann and hugged her tight. Ann took the embrace, because she needed it. It was nice to be in her mother's arms after Rex's words. She wanted to rush home, but both she and her mother treasured their time together, so she stuck it out. He wouldn't be back in now. He'd had the last word, and that was all that mattered to him. She knew that from past experience with him.

They had lunch and talked about plans for the week to come. Amanda joined in, one of the family, not a servant, no matter what the servants said. She had to follow what James told her, he would report her to the aliens if not, but if Mary asked for her, he couldn't complain. She was the head of the household, not James.

She had started to smile again by the time she was ready to head home. She needed to take a shower to get rid of the headache her tears had caused and get dressed for dinner. Rager was a soldier, but he liked to look nice when they ate, and she'd automatically followed suit.

"You come back any time, baby girl. You know you always have a place to come home to, if you need it," Mary said as she hugged Anne goodbye.

"I know, Mom. I love you."

"I love you, Ann. Now get home to that mate of yours." Mary brushed some of Ann's brown hair behind her ear with a tender smile, and then kissed her cheek. "See you soon."

"Bye, Mom." Ann waved at her Mom as she got into her transporter, a smile still in place. That smile froze when she glanced at the side of the house. Rex was there, and he wasn't alone.

Some pretty, little blond wolf girl leaned against the

side of the house, her eyes wide and adoring as she looked up at Rex. Her Rex! But not anymore. He cast his eyes at Ann, long enough for her to see he knew she was there, and then he leaned down to kiss the girl, and not in a brotherly way. He pulled her hips close to his as he kissed her, and she didn't fight him at all.

If he'd wanted to drive home his point, then he'd just done that. It hurt, but not because he was kissing someone else. It hurt because he wanted to hurt her. That he'd done all of that deliberately.

She might have been forced to mate with Rager, but he knew that. Even if he wanted to believe now that she'd chosen to be mated to Rager, he knew better. They all did. And he took out his contrived anger on her, like a child!

She let a sneer spread over her face, raised her left eyebrow, and sat down in her transporter. Maybe it wasn't so bad she'd escaped him, she decided. She'd felt bad since she'd been mated to Rager. Now? Well, now she knew she was nothing more than a pawn, but she didn't feel so bad about how much she adored Rager's attentions.

Rex only wanted her because he was playing with her, the way a cat would a mouse. She could see that now. She'd been little more than a toy to him.

To be fair, she kind of felt the same way about Rager. He'd wanted someone to play house with, someone to play at husband and wife, like some 1950s TV show. He'd found a way to force her into it, despite his claim he didn't know she didn't want to be mated to him.

There was nothing she could do about it now, she knew. She didn't want to stop being his mate. He made her feel alive and like she was heading straight for death, all in the same breathtaking moment, and it was amazing. She'd been drawn to him, even before they'd been mated, her body had known that he was the man for her.

There'd been no talk of love, she thought as she pointed herself home, but it was growing. She knew it must be. He was so tender with her, so kind. Yes, she was a toy for him, but she thought she saw love in his eyes, sometimes, when he wasn't aware she had her eyes on him. The way he'd curl around her when they slept, as if to keep her safe, was also sweet, but something she knew he must not be aware of. It was unconscious, the body's need to protect someone, even when that body was asleep.

That wouldn't happen if she was just a body for him to fuck. She meant something to him. Not like Rex, who'd never really cared. He'd just wanted to get between her legs. She could see that now. He'd wanted what he couldn't have. And she'd played his game for far too long.

She could report him to Rager, make him pay for his

treatment of her, but that would hurt his parents. And hers. And her.

She was sad, more than anything, she decided later when she climbed into the shower. Sad at the way their lives had turned out. All those months ago, they thought salvation was at hand. For a moment, Ann had even wondered about faith and stories she'd never quite believed in.

They hadn't known that the aliens brought them a new life, a life full of riches, but also, a life full of sorrow. Tears slid down her eyes again, and she longed for her old MP3 player. She'd love to hear those old songs again. Those songs knew her pain, pain she hadn't understood until now.

They'd thought they were going to be the new masters of the universe, that the world was theirs to take. How little they'd known. The aliens, with a name none of the people on Earth could pronounce, or spell, had given and taken away.

Ann hated the racism against the wolves but knew there was little she could do. She'd start to work on her mate, try to talk to him about their treatment, but there was little else she could do.

She was a woman of privilege now, she had things the rest of the Earth wouldn't see for generations. She had choices, so many choices. But choosing which dinner to have that night didn't compare to the ability to choose whether people were slaves or not. The choice between a green dress and a blue one was inconsequential, when she couldn't even decide who to be mated to.

She couldn't even choose her own vocabulary now, she thought as she turned the water off in the shower. Mated to. Not her husband, not who she'd married, but who she was mated to. It was all so… stupid.

Somehow, she would change this, she would change it all. She would make this brand-new world a better place. If Rager was the supreme leader of the world now, then that meant there could be pockets of people all over. She would find a way to make sure they all, wolf and non-wolf, were given the choices that mattered. And hopefully, in the process, she'd come to terms with all that had happened to her.

More than that, she hoped she could find a way to stop Rex before he ruined it for them all. Somehow, she had to stop his blind hatred of Rager and his people. And now her. She was a traitor in his eyes, and she knew now there was nothing she could do to change it. She just hoped he didn't go off the deep end.

ABOUT THE AUTHOR

Selina Coffey is a romance writer who lives happily in London with her husband and son. She is a hopeless romantic who grew up always believing in love and she is not ashamed to admit this! It is this belief that makes her so passionate about writing crazy love stories.

A stereotypical girly girl, she loves shopping. So whenever she gets a chance and the spare cash, you will probably find her browsing online for the next pair of shoes to add to her collection!

You can find her online at
www.selinacoffey.com

Contact her at
hello@selinacoffey.com